Tales of a
Chinese Grandmother

BY FRANCES CARPENTER

TALES OF A CHINESE GRANDMOTHER

TALES OF A KOREAN GRANDMOTHER

TALES OF A
Chinese Grandmother

by
FRANCES CARPENTER

illustrated by
MALTHE HASSELRIIS

CHARLES E. TUTTLE COMPANY
Rutland, Vermont & Tokyo, Japan

Representatives
Continental Europe: BOXERBOOKS, INC., *Zurich*
British Isles: PRENTICE-HALL INTERNATIONAL, INC., *London*
Australasia: PAUL FLESCH & CO., PTY. LTD., *Melbourne*
Canada: HURTIG PUBLISHERS, *Edmonton*

Published by the Charles E. Tuttle Company, Inc.
of Rutland, Vermont & Tokyo, Japan
with editorial offices at
Suido 1-chome, 2-6, Bunkyo-ku, Tokyo, Japan

Copyright in Japan, 1973, by Charles E. Tuttle Co., Inc.

Library of Congress Catalog Card No. 72-77514

International Standard Book No. 0-8048-1042-7

First edition, 1937
by Doubleday & Company, Inc., New York
First Tuttle edition, 1973
Second printing, 1975

0297-000323-4615
PRINTED IN JAPAN

TO MY FATHER

FRANK G. CARPENTER

TABLE OF CONTENTS

vii

LIST OF ILLUSTRATIONS

ACKNOWLEDGMENT

THE POPULAR FOLK TALES which have been adapted in this book by the author, have been collected from many sources, among which mention should be made of E. T. C. Werner's "Myths and Legends of China" and "A Dictionary of Chinese Mythology"; Dr. John C. Ferguson's "Chinese Mythology"; *The China Review;* Edouard Chavannes "Cinq Cents Contes et Apologues, Extraits du Tripitaka Chinois"; Herbert A. Giles' translation of the tales of P'u Sung-ling; General Tcheng Ki-tong's "Les Plaisirs en China"; and Wang Chi Chen's translation of "The Dream of the Red Chamber."

The author also wishes to express gratitude to Jen Tai, Chinese poet and critic, for assistance in checking the accuracy of her pictures of family life in Old China.

xi

Tales of a
Chinese Grandmother

Tales of a
Chinese Grandmother

I

INSIDE THE BRIGHT RED GATE

THE TWO HALVES of the bright red gate in the gray wall
had been opened for the day. Old Chang, the blue-gowned
gatekeeper of the Ling household, had already wiped
clean the glossy red varnish that covered their wood
sides. He was now busy polishing the brass bird-heads
from whose beaks hung heavy rings that served as gate
handles.

"The Old Mistress will come soon. The gate must be i

order," the man muttered to himself as he slowly rubbed the yellow metal.

Outside, along the narrow street of the Chinese city, between the gray walls that rose high on each side of it, men were passing back and forth on their early morning errands. Inside this red gate people were stirring. All the low one-story houses built round the Ling courtyards were coming to life.

In one of the inner courts two children, a boy named Ah Shung, and his sister, Yu Lang, stood before a door that opened upon a covered veranda under a curving roof of gray tiles.

"We are here, bowing before you, Grandmother," the boy said as he rapped on the wooden door frame.

"Are you well, Lao Lao?" asked the girl who was standing just behind him.

"Ai, Little Bear. Ai, my precious Jade Flower, it is you. Have you eaten already?" a voice called from within.

The two children bowed low as the old woman came to the door and stood there for a moment looking them over. Ah Shung and Yu Lang admired their grandmother. She was the oldest and thus the most important person they knew. In their land, where age was treated with such great respect, everyone wished to be thought as old as possible. The name their grandmother liked best to be called was "Lao Lao," which means "Old Old One."

In her elegant garments of dark silk lined with soft squirrel fur this old Chinese grandmother made a fine figure. She was not very tall, but from the tip of her carefully combed gray hair to the tiny points of her wee satin shoes she seemed to the children the very picture of a great lady.

Lao Lao was wearing a short coat, all of plum color with a beautiful pattern of flowers woven in its silk threads. Her long blue skirt almost covered the loose fur-lined silk pantaloons which she had on underneath. Her embroidered satin shoes, which could just be seen below her heavy silk skirt, were not more than four or five inches long, for her feet had been squeezed into tight stiff bindings after the old Chinese fashion. A gold pin was thrust through the coil of gray hair that lay flat against her neck, carved pieces of precious green jade-stone hung from her ears, and gold bracelets and rings adorned her hands and her wrists.

As she looked at her grandchildren the old woman's slanting eyes sparkled with pleasure. Her strong, kindly face lighted up as she asked them about the breakfast they had just eaten in the family hall.

Ah Shung and Yu Lang were handsome Chinese children. Their skin was creamy yellow and their black eyes were set aslant above their high cheekbones. They were well dressed, as was proper for children of the wealthy Ling family. Both wore their black hair long, in neat braids down their backs. These children lived many years ago, before new ways came to the Flowery Kingdom of China. In those old days all Chinese men and boys, as well as young girls, wore their hair in such long braids or queues. Ah

Shung's forehead was shaved high and smooth, while his sister's brow was hidden by a straight fringe of hair cut square above her slanting black eyes. Near its end the little girl's shining black braid was wound neatly for several inches with some bright scarlet thread.

The coming of winter had brought with it the "Small Cold," as the Chinese sometimes call the first chilly days. About the doors and the windows, cracks in the houses had been sealed up with paper to keep out the cold winds. Fires were burning under the brick beds and in little brass or iron stoves set out in the rooms. But these did not give nearly enough warmth, so everyone had put on several suits of thick clothing.

Both Ah Shung and Yu Lang had on short jackets and long trousers of thick wadded cotton. The little girl's pantaloons hung loose about her tiny feet, while her brother's were wrapped tightly about his ankles, just above his shoes of dark cloth. Over his padded suits Ah Shung had on a long gown of heavy blue cloth, and on top of this a short jacket of black. Yu Lang's outer garments were of padded silk of gay colors. Her pantaloons were leaf green and her jacket bright blue. Like her grandmother's, the little girl's feet were tightly bound up so as to make them seem small.

"Call Fu," the old woman said to her maid, Huang Ying, who was helping her down the two stone steps that led out into the courtyard. "I am ready to look to the household. Ah Shung and Yu Lang may walk beside us as we go."

"Fu is here, Aged and Honorable Lady," said a soft voice at her side. A tall man stood before her, bowing respectfully, his hands at his sides. It was Fu, the number one servant, who had charge of all the men and women who tended the wants of this family of Ling. Each of the other servants looked up to Fu because he knew how to read and even to write a little. The only one who thought herself more important than Fu was old Wang Lai, the number one nurse. She had cared for the father of Ah Shung and Yu Lang when he was a child, and she always let people know that she had served the Ling family even longer than Fu.

Inside the bright red gate Grandmother Ling ruled like an empress. Every few days, leaning heavily upon the arm of one of her maids, she would toddle on her bound feet through the courtyards which lay one behind the other inside the high gray walls. She looked into every corner, for, as she used to say to the children, "When the mistress shuts her eye, the maids fall asleep."

At the red gate the Old Mistress, as the servants called her, stopped to chat with Chang, the gatekeeper. They stood out of the wind, behind a tall screen made of bricks which faced the red gate and sheltered the entrance court from the curious gazes of passers-by. Ah Shung and Yu Lang ran around to the street side of the screen. They wanted to look at the painted green dragon that twisted and turned across its broad face. The huge beast seemed to be trying to catch in his claws a round scarlet ball which their grandmother told them was meant to be a flaming pearl.

"That wall keeps off the bad spirits that fly about us through the air," Ah Shung explained for the thousandth time to his sister. "The Old Old One says the spirits that ride on the wind have to go straight. They cannot turn corners. So when bad spirits fly in through the red gate, they meet this strong screen. They must go back. And the sight of our good dragon sends them flying out faster than they came in."

Grandmother Ling and many other Chinese believed in spirits, both good and bad. They took greatest care to protect themselves from them. To be doubly safe, this family had set up a second spirit screen inside the round Moon Gate that led from the entrance yard to the courtyard beyond it.

The Old Mistress inspected the entrance court carefully. She looked at the houses on each side of the red gate where Chang and some of the other men servants lived. She peered into the near-by courts where the horses and traveling carts were kept and where several little two-wheeled carriages called "jinrikishas" were lined up, waiting until the men of the family should wish to go out. She talked with the sturdy riksha men, each of whom trotted as fast as a horse between the shafts of his small carriage when he pulled it along smoothly over the streets of the city.

Ah Shung and Yu Lang followed their grandmother through the Moon Gate, the round opening cut in the lower white wall that separated the entrance court from the courtyard beyond. They made their way around the white spirit screen there and then crossed the paved courtyard. Bits of green grass were growing up between the gray paving bricks, and huge china flowerpots, filled with dwarf evergreens, lined the way to the steps of the gray one-story houses that were built with verandas upon the open square.

The children admired especially the low brick building that faced the Moon Gate. This was the hall where important guests were received. Its roof of gray tiles was more gracefully curved at the corners and its latticework windows, backed with white paper to let in the light, were more beautifully made than those of any of the other houses inside the red gate. Little wind bells that hung under its eaves tinkled in the strong breeze. The smaller houses on either side of this courtyard served as library and study for the men of the family. Ah Shung and Yu Lang always behaved particularly well when they were called to meet visitors in this Courtyard of Politeness.

The two children felt more at home in the second courtyard beyond the entrance court. This was the first of the family courts. In its central building was the hall where everyone gathered for meals and where close friends were received. Here Grandmother Ling had her own apartment, and on one side were the rooms of some of the older children of the family. A house on the left in this courtyard was given over to the parents of Ah Shung and Yu Lang, and the children themselves occupied, with their nurse, the low building along its other side. Their father was the oldest son of Grandmother Ling. So, of course, he had a better house on a more important court than his younger brothers, who lived with their wives and their children in the two smaller courts behind.

The Ling household was large. As was the custom, all the grown-up sons and their families lived here together inside the same walls. Many servants were needed for so many masters. Indeed, such great numbers of people lived inside the Ling gate that it seemed almost like a town.

"Sky-well" is the meaning of one Chinese name for a courtyard such as those where Ah Shung and his sister passed their days and their nights. No doubt the Chinese give it this name because the courtyard is so shut in by houses and walls that the only outside thing to be seen is the sky overhead.

There were many gray brick houses built around the Ling sky-wells. There was the Hall of the Ancestors where, this family believed, the spirits of their forefathers dwelt, their own special places shown by little red tablets of wood, each marked with a name in glistening gold. There was the schoolhouse where Scholar Shih, the family teacher, lived and where all the children inside the red gate had their daily lessons. There was the house where the men-cooks prepared the family food, and then there were all the small houses where the men and the maid servants slept.

"We shall end our walk in the Garden of Sweet Smells,"

said Grandmother Ling as they went through a gate, shaped like a flower vase, cut in the white wall. Giving orders to the number one gardener, the old woman walked slowly along its neat little paths, over a tiny humpbacked bridge of white stone that rose above the pool where dragon-eyed goldfish with long flowing tails were swimming about in the clear water. She noted some rocks sliding out of their places in the tiny mountain that had been built up in the center of the garden, and she found that a tile had fallen from the roof of the garden pavilion where the family often drank tea on warm summer days.

"Go now to the schoolmaster, Ah Shung," Lao Lao commanded as she came again to her own courtyard. "A boy who does not learn is like a knife with a dull edge. See that you work well. And you, Precious Pearl," she said to Yu Lang, "come with me for an hour with the embroidery needle."

The boy and his sister did not see each other again until the midday meal. Then all the Ling family came together. At midday, and again each evening, the great family hall rang with their chatter and laughter as they took their places about the tables. At the family table Grandmother Ling sat in the place of honor. Her chair was just in front of a high narrow side table of shining carved wood. Upon this, between two tall scarlet candles, stood the statue of the Chinese Goddess of Mercy, whose name is Gwan Yin. From painted scrolls, hung upon the gray wall above her head, two of the Ling forefathers, dressed in rich robes of red and blue, looked down with calm faces upon the family gathered beneath them. About the table with its red cloth sat Grandmother Ling's three sons and their wives and their older children. Ah Shung and Yu Lang and their younger cousins from the other courts ate with the nurses at smaller tables at the sides of the room.

Maid servants moved to and fro, bringing bowls of steaming white rice and dish after dish of meat and salted vegetables to eat with it. There was chicken, pork, and fish, turnips, carrots, and cabbage, and a kind of bean cheese. All these different foods were lifted from the thin blue eating bowls with the two little sticks which served these children instead of forks. Foreigners call these Chinese eating-sticks "chopsticks." This really means "quick sticks."

"We come to the table to eat, not to carve," Grandmother Ling would say when someone told her of the queer customs of other lands, where people used knives and forks. So all the food of this household was cut up into small pieces before it was set on the table. Grandmother Ling used her own little chopsticks of ivory and silver like a pair of tongs. She picked up her food daintily and she popped it into her mouth without losing a grain of rice or a drop of good sauce.

Ah Shung and Yu Lang ate quickly. Their chopsticks of bamboo flew back and forth between their bowls and their mouths. They ate a great deal at breakfast, as well as at midday and in the evening. At four in the afternoon they had an extra meal of tea and steaming hot dumplings. Grandmother Ling would have thought they were ill if they had not stuffed themselves full or if they had laid down their chopsticks before their rice bowls were empty.

The Old Old One often had special food served to her in order to give her the strength she needed in her old age. She liked swallow's-nest soup, flavored with the sticky gum with which these birds put their nests together. She sometimes had a stew made from a certain kind of chicken whose bones were black as coal. Into this stew she liked to sift some powdered deer's horn which she thought an excellent tonic. White peony root, chopped very fine and cooked with the chicken, made it even better. As a relish she often ate pickled eggs, that had been kept so many years that they had turned to black jelly; and the tea with which she quenched her thirst was flavored with jasmine flowers.

Nothing was too fine for the Old Mistress. She came first with everyone inside the red gate. Since their father was dead, her grown-up sons asked her advice about everything they did, and they even received their spending money from her. Grandmother Ling had as much to do with the children as their own mothers. They learned more in the hours they spent at her side than they did in the schoolroom.

Ah Shung and Yu Lang were very fond of their grandmother. No one knew so many splendid stories as she. When she was a child her father had had her taught to read and to write just like her brothers. With her soft rabbit-hair brush and the sweet-smelling black paste upon her ink stone she could make even more beautiful Chinese words than Scholar Shih, who was now teaching the children to write. She could read from the paper books, with their delicate covers and their soft pages filled with up-and-down rows of strange black word pictures.

After their evening meal the Lings sat for a time drinking bowls of hot liquid which had the same delicate color as a yellow-green bamboo leaf. This was their tea, which they took instead of water.

"We are to go into Lao Lao's room tonight," Ah Shung said to his sister and cousins as he emptied his tea bowl. The boy's black eyes glistened. He liked nothing better than the family gatherings in his grandmother's apartment when often poems were read and stories were told.

Grandmother Ling knew many tales about dragons and unicorns, about firebirds, or phoenixes, that were born in the sun, and the Heavenly Dog that tried to swallow the moon. She knew about spirits that ruled the wind and the water. She knew about foxes that turned into people, and about the Jade Rabbit that dwelt in the moon. Gods that flew up to heaven, men who lived forever, and beautiful maidens from the Heavenly Kingdom were found in her stories.

In the days when Ah Shung and Yu Lang dwelt inside the red gate of the Lings', the Chinese people really believed in spirits and gods and such fairy-tale creatures. Even today many Chinese are not sure that they do not exist. Lao Lao, who told these strange stories, and these children, who listened, had never a doubt but that they were true.

II

HOW PAN KU MADE THE WORLD

You may offer my guests ginger, Ah Shung, and you may offer sugared lotus seed, Yu Lang," Grandmother Ling said to the children when the family gathered in her room after the evening meal. Huang Ying, the old woman's

14

favorite maid servant, went to a tall mahogany cabinet
that stood against the wall, and from its carved wooden
shelf she lifted down a small blue-and-white bowl which she
put into the boy's hands. She gave to Yu Lang a china jar
with a scene on its sides done in all the five colors: red, yellow, blue, black, and white.

The children held these out politely in both their hands.
They bowed as they offered them to the Old Old One, who
sat very straight in her great chair of carved polished
wood. Then they bowed before the other grownups, who
selected bits of orange-colored ginger and some sugary
seeds with their thin yellow fingers.

The men in their long gowns of dark silk were seated
near their wives, with little tables beside them, the eldest
having places of honor nearest Lao Lao. With their shining black hair coiled so neatly upon their necks, with their
smooth faces so carefully tinted with red and white powder,
and with their gowns of fine silk and embroidery, the
younger women looked like the delicate figures on Lao
Lao's best summer fan.

Across the back of this room, framed in carved wood,
was Grandmother Ling's brick bed under which a fire
burned. Her soft silken comforters were piled upon it out
of the way in the corner, and the green curtains that hung
from under its canopy were pushed aside. Upon the warm
floor of the bed sat some of the other children with their
feet tucked beneath them. They greeted the ginger and the
lotus seeds with the broadest of smiles, but they took care

not to seem to be in a hurry to take them lest they should be thought impolite.

"It is the hour for our Little Dragon to go to sleep," said Grandmother Ling. She looked toward the small boy whose name, Lung-Er, had been given him in the hope that he would grow up to be as strong and as good as a mighty dragon. Also, when they heard this name the bad spirits might think he was not a child at all but a young dragon whom they would not dare to carry away.

Lung-Er was only three years old. He was the youngest of all the Ling children and the pet of everyone, big and little, inside the red gate. Around his neck he wore a silver chain fastened with a silver lock, bought with coins given by one hundred friends of the family. The Lings firmly believed this would chain him to earth. A red string was twined in his tiny black braid to bring him good luck.

The little boy was bundled up in thick padded clothing. In his outer suit of gay red he looked just like the fat top that Ah Shung often spun on the hard floor of his room. Everyone laughed as Lung-Er stood before his grandmother and made such a low bow that he almost toppled over.

"He grows," said Grandmother Ling, smiling, as his nurse took the child away. "He grows almost as fast as Pan Ku, who made the world."

Ah Shung and Yu Lang hurried to bring their stools close to their grandmother's chair. They looked up into her face with such eager expressions that the old woman laughed.

"Ho, these two want a story about the mighty Pan Ku! Well, it will do no harm for us to hear that tale once again," she said as she wiped the sugar from her wrinkled fingers on a damp towel which Huang Ying held for her.

"Once long, long ago," she began, "there was no world. But from somewhere or other there came this man called Pan Ku. With his hammer and a cutting tool, called a "chisel," he began to make the earth. Each day Pan Ku grew six feet in height. The earth grew just as fast. With his head Pan Ku pushed the sky farther and farther away. He made the earth larger and larger.

"From out of the sky four beasts came to help him. There was the good unicorn with his single great horn growing out of his forehead and his hairy hide with all the five colors upon it. His body was shaped like a deer's, but his hoofs were those of a horse. His tail was like that of an ox, and his horn was tipped with a tuft of soft flesh.

"And there was the phoenix, the king of the birds, who came from the sun. On his body, too, there were all the five colors, and his tail had twelve feathers, one for each moon of the year. Such long feathers they were that they trailed far behind him as he flew through the air.

"The great tortoise that lived for thousands of years also aided Pan Ku. But best of all there was a dragon so huge that he could reach all the way across the broad sky. Pan Ku's dragon may have looked like those that are carved upon my bed."

The children examined anew the carved wooden dragons that served as legs for the frame of the Old Old One's bed. Each of the twisting creatures had a head like a cow, the body of a serpent, scales like a fish, feet round as a tiger's paw, and claws like an eagle's. Two short horns were on its head, and its eyes popped from their sockets. Its wide mouth was open, and a slender tongue was thrust out between its long fangs.

"What did Pan Ku look like, Lao Lao?" Ah Shung asked as his grandmother paused for a moment. In reply the old woman sent her maid, Huang Ying, to bring a scroll from the carved cabinet.

"Here is Pan Ku," Grandmother Ling said as she unrolled the strip of silk and paper that was wound about a shiny black stick. "This is an old painting that belonged to your grandfather. How long it has been in the Ling treasure chests nobody knows."

Everyone gathered about as the old picture was spread out on the floor and weights were laid on its corners. Strangely enough, this Pan Ku was not tall, but Lao Lao explained that the artist might have been showing him before he began to grow so quickly. Two little horns were set upon his wrinkled brow, and an apron of green leaves was his only garment. In one hand he carried his hammer and in the other his chisel. And near by, at his feet, were his helpers, the unicorn and the dragon, the phoenix and the tortoise.

"Nothing that is done hastily is well done, my children. So it is not at all strange that it took Pan Ku eighteen thousand years to finish making the world." Grandmother Ling went on with her story. "But at last the sky was round and the earth was ready. There was no living thing on it, however, until Pan Ku died and his spirit flew away to the Heavenly Kingdom. He gave life to the world. His head became its high mountains. His breath became the winds that blew over it and the clouds that crossed the sky. His voice rolled in the thunder. The blood in his veins turned into rivers, his flesh made the fields, and his skin and his hair made the plants and the trees. His eyes became stars, and his sweat made the rain. Tiny insects that crawled upon his great body were changed into live men and women. And so the world began."

"What about the sun and the moon, Aged and Honorable Mother?" Ah Shung's father inquired. He had heard this story many times, but he enjoyed watching the wondering faces of the younger children who listened so eagerly.

"Oh, the sun and the moon," the old woman said. "Like Pan Ku, I forgot them. Pan Ku neglected to set them in the sky where they belonged. The earth was in darkness. There was no day. There was no night. The emperor who ruled the first people tried to summon the sun and the moon from under the sea where they were hiding. He sent a messenger to them. But no ray of light broke through the darkness.

"There was nothing to do but to call Pan Ku back from the Heavenly Kingdom. Upon the palm of his left hand he drew the sign of the sun, and upon the palm of his right hand he marked the sign of the moon. In turn he stretched his hands out toward the sea. Seven times he called the sun and moon to come forth. He commanded them to take their places up in the sky. Even the sun and the moon could not disobey the mighty Pan Ku. In chariots drawn by strong dragons they rose from the water. Light flooded the heavens, and day and night came to the world.

"I have heard it told that Pan Ku appeared upon the earth once again," said Grandmother Ling. "For many hundreds of years his spirit had no home in the other world. Like all poor homeless spirits, it rode hither and yon upon the strong winds. Then at last it came upon a woman who dwelt on a mountain so high that it was only a step from its top to the Heavenly Kingdom. This woman was a remarkable creature who filled her stomach with clouds and who quenched her thirst with the light from the sun and the moon.

"Well, the spirit of Pan Ku chose to enter the body of this woman's baby. As I heard the tale, her wonderful child could stand up and walk about and speak words of wisdom from the very first moment at which he entered the world. Wherever he went a five-colored cloud floated around him.

"When he grew old again Pan Ku took refuge upon the high Eastern Mountain. As he sat at the door of his cave in the rocks the five-colored clouds still hung over his head. Because of his great age and because of his wisdom, pilgrims came from afar to hear his good words. It was the old god of that Eastern Mountain who found out who he was. He made a special journey to visit the Emperor of Heaven, and from him he learned that the wise hermit of the Eastern Mountain was really Pan Ku, who made the world with his hammer and chisel in the very beginning."

III

THE SISTERS IN THE SUN

As grandmother ling finished the story of Pan Ku she called for her water pipe. Her maid, Huang Ying, fetched the pipe and set it down on a low stool beside the Old Mistress. She lighted the tobacco in its little bowl. The Old Old One drew in her breath. She liked the taste of the tobacco smoke that passed through the water in the body of the pipe on its way to her mouth.

"Who lives in the sun, Lao Lao?" Ah Shung asked his grandmother as she puffed away at her pipe.

"No one knows but the gods in the sky, Little Bear,"

the old woman replied. "Some say it is a golden raven, and that that is why our sign for the sun is that bird inside a circle. But the sun is not like the moon, my children. We can sometimes see the people who live in the moon. You yourself have seen the Moon Rabbit and the toad on the moon's face. And I have often thought I could see the Moon Lady, Heng O. But who can look at the sun? Ai, there is a tale about that. Would you like to hear it?" Grandmother Ling looked about the circle. Everyone was listening to her with the greatest of interest.

"Ah, Excellent One of Great Age and Wisdom," her oldest son said, "brighten our dark minds with the light of your learning. Tell us more."

"Well then, my old nurse used to say that in ancient days a young man lived in the sun, while his two younger sisters dwelt in the moon. The two maidens were beautiful, more beautiful even than the fairest blooms in our garden. Slender as the bamboo they were, and as graceful as willow branches swayed by the breeze. Their faces were shaped like the oval seed of a melon, and the black of their eyes was circled with white as pure as new snow. Their eyebrows were like the clear outline of some distant mountain, and their feet were as small as the buds of the lily.

"These two sisters were clever with the embroidery needle. With their thin pointed fingers they stitched the flowers and the dragons, the birds and the butterflies, that adorned their silk robes. They covered each of their tiny shoes with twenty thousand fine stitches. All night they

All night the two sisters could be seen in their palace garden, stitching away by the light of the moon

could be seen in their palace garden, stitching away by the light of the moon.

"The fame of the beauty of the sisters in the moon spread over the land. Each clear night people gathered in their gardens and climbed the high mountains to gaze up at the moon for a sight of their loveliness. From their palace in the sky the moon sisters could see clearly what went on upon the earth so far down below them.

"Now these sisters knew well the rules for maidenly conduct. Like all Chinese girls they had been taught that it was not fitting that men should gaze upon them. Each night, as more and more people stared up at the moon, they became more and more unhappy.

" 'We cannot stay here, my sister,' said one of the moon maidens at last.

" 'I have thought of a plan,' said the other as she embroidered the tail of a dragon on the front of her new robe. 'We shall go away from here. We shall change homes with our brother. He shall live here in the moon and we shall take his place in the sun.'

"The moon maidens put on their handsomest red robes and went to seek help from their brother in the sun.

" 'O Venerable Brother,' they said when they came to his shining palace, 'we are in great trouble and only you can help us. Each night, down on earth, people gaze up at the moon and their eyes fall upon us. That should not be. We are very unhappy.'

"The brother who lived in the sun was as distressed as

his sisters, but he laughed when they told him they wished to live in the sun.

" 'Silly creatures,' he scoffed, 'in the daytime when the sun shines in the sky there are a hundred times more people abroad than there are in the night, when the moon can be seen. You will have more eyes than ever upon you if you change places with me.'

" 'Ai-yah, Honorable Brother,' they cried, 'if you will but change with us, indeed all will be well. Into our un-worthy minds the gods have sent a plan which we are sure will succeed.'

"The maidens wept. The brother was fond of his sisters and at last he agreed to change places with them. He left his palace in the sun and took up his abode in the moon. Joyfully the sisters gathered together their beautiful robes and their other belongings. They did not forget to pack in a shining red chest their embroidery silks and their seventy needles. In less than the time it takes to drink a cup of tea they were comfortably settled in the sun palace.

"Down on the earth when men could no longer see the sisters in the moon, they wondered. 'The moon princesses have disappeared!' they exclaimed. 'A man sits there in their place. Where can they have gone?' Then somehow or other the word went around that the beautiful maidens now lived in the sun.

"But the sisters' plan worked. They were safe at last from the eyes of the people on earth. For as soon as anyone turned his gaze full on the sun he felt tiny pricking pains in his eyes. Some said that it was only the strong rays of the sun. But my nurse always declared that it was the seventy embroidery needles of the two beautiful sisters, who pricked the eyes of any person who was so bold as to stare at them."

Ah Shung and Yu Lang looked at each other. Only that day they had dared each other to gaze straight at the sun. They had found out for themselves what the pricking of the sun sisters' needles felt like in their eyes.

"Ai, the sun is our friend," Grandmother Ling told her grandchildren between her puffs at her bubbling water pipe. "I remember one time when the Heavenly Dog almost ate the sun up. How frightened we were! I was about the age of Yu Lang when it happened, but I can still see it all with the mirror of my mind."

The old woman was remembering a day when the moon passed between the sun and the earth and for a few minutes shut off its light. We should call that an eclipse, but the Chinese believed that the sky dog which lived upon a certain star was trying to swallow the sun.

"The Son of Heaven, our Emperor, sent forth a warning from his dragon throne," said the Old Old One. "From the soothsayers he had learned that the sun was to be eaten, and he told us what to do. Well I remember the day. All the servants inside our walls, and indeed in all the courts of the city, brought forth drums and brass cymbals, rattles and pans. We kept watch, and as soon as the sun began to disappear down the throat of the wicked dog of the sky they beat on the drums. They whirled the rattles and they knocked on the pans. They clashed the brass cymbals together. What a noise they did make! I grew frightened and cried and hid behind my old nurse. Ai-yah, the sky dog almost succeeded in swallowing the sun that time. It grew very dark, and only a rim of light showed in the heavens. The servants beat the drums harder. The cymbals clashed louder. At last the sky dog took fright. He coughed up the sun, which shone bright again in its place overhead in the sky."

IV

GENTLE GWAN YIN

IT WAS THE EIGHTH DAY of the cold Twelfth Moon. A film of ice covered the goldfish pool in the bare Garden of Sweet Smells. Lines of fine white snow lay between the broad paving bricks of all the courtyards within the red gate. In the family hall a little fire of glowing balls of coal dust burned in the iron stove on the floor near the Old Mistress' chair.

The Ling family was gathered beside the tables with their red cloths already spread for the midday meal. All eyes were fixed upon Grandmother Ling. The old woman, in one of her finest gray silken gowns, walked to the high narrow table of shining carved wood which was placed against the back wall of the hall. With slow, careful movements she lighted the incense sticks in the brass burner upon it. A spicy smell drifted through the room as the smoke rose and floated in a thin blue cloud about the gilded statue that stood in the center of the table.

"On this day of the year the gentle Gwan Yin left the world behind her and went to dwell with the holy women in the Nunnery of the White Sparrow," old Wang Lai, the nurse, had told Ah Shung and Yu Lang as they came across the courtyard to the family hall.

Yu Lang thought that this statue of Gwan Yin, the Chiness Goddess of Mercy, was the most precious thing in all the Ling houses. Its gilded wood carving showed a slender woman, holding a baby close to her breast. Her face was calm and kind as well as beautiful. Her long flowing robes swirled about her feet, which were set upon the heart of a lotus blossom.

Huang Ying, the maid, steadied the Old Mistress as she got down on her knees before the likeness of Gwan Yin. Lao Lao bent her head and swayed forward and back, forward and back, forward and back. This way of showing respect is known as a "kowtow." Grandmother Ling said a little prayer each time she bowed. Then the other members of the family kowtowed in their turn before the gilt statue.

"There is la-pa-chou in our bowls today," Ah Shung whispered to Yu Lang when the children took their places at the table. They were especially fond of this dish, which was always served on this particular day. They often counted upon their fingers all the good things in it. Five kinds of grain, beans, peanuts and chestnuts, walnuts and dates, lily and melon seeds, several different fruits, as well as sugar and spices! Twenty different things were always mixed together to make Gwan Yin's porridge.

"Truly there is no stove so powerful as a full stomach," said Grandmother Ling as she laid her ivory and silver chopsticks across her empty bowl. She sat back in her chair with a sigh of content.

"Let the children come nearer," the old woman commanded, "and I will tell them the story of the gentle Gwan Yin.

"In earliest times, my little ones, there lived an Emperor whose name was Po Chia. With his Empress he ruled the land wisely and well. But because of some wrongdoing of the past the gods sent them no sons. There was no one to sit upon the dragon throne when Po Chia should be called to be a guest in heaven.

"So Po Chia and his lady went to the far Western Mountain, and they prayed to the god there to give them a child. Their prayers were answered. Three children were born but, ai, all the three were daughters.

" 'We so much needed a son,' the poor Empress wailed. 'Three candles do not take the place of one lamp.'

" 'Well, it cannot be helped,' said the Emperor Po Chia. 'Our daughters will marry, and one of their husbands shall become Emperor when I go to dwell in the World of Shadows.'

"The Emperor's favorite daughter was the youngest, who was then called Miao Shan. Since Po Chia loved her best he decided that her husband should become Emperor after him, and that thus she should become the Empress. But the maid, Miao Shan, did not wish to marry.

" 'I know that it is wicked to disobey my honorable father,' she said, 'but the glory of being an Empress is like the light of the moon reflected in a stream. Morning comes and it is gone. I only wish to sit quiet and pray to the gods that I may become perfect. I wish to care for the sick and to help the poor. I do not wish to marry.'

"The Emperor Po Chia was so angry that he ordered the guards to take away Miao Shan's fine clothes. 'Let her be cast out into the garden where she may die of hunger and cold,' he commanded. But the winds brought the good princess food, and the moon warmed her with its light.

"The court ladies, her sisters, and even the Emperor and the Empress themselves came to beg her to change her mind. But the maiden refused. She asked that she might be allowed to leave her father's palace and go to live with the good women who shut themselves away from the world in the Nunnery of the White Sparrow.

" 'Let her go to the nunnery,' the Emperor commanded, 'but send word to the mistress that she be given the hardest tasks and that she be discouraged from becoming a nun.'

"Poor Miao Shan was set to work in the nunnery kitchen. She was made to scrub floors and to carry great pails of water. She set herself to her tasks without a complaint. But, my children, the Emperor of Heaven looked down and took pity upon her. He sent dragons to carry her water, a tiger to bring her wood, and birds to gather vegetables for her from the garden. Spirits scrubbed the floors for her and did all the hard work.

"When he heard of the wonderful happenings at the Nunnery of the White Sparrow, the Emperor grew more angry than before. He ordered his troops to surround it and to burn its buildings down to the ground.

"But the smoke from the fire they made carried up to Heaven the prayers of the good Miao Shan. At once clouds gathered in the sky and torrents of rain fell upon the flames, putting them out.

" 'Go back! Seize my daughter! Put her in chains and cut off her head!' the angry Emperor commanded when he heard of that happening.

"But the Empress, who loved her daughter, begged for her life. 'O Wise Son of Heaven,' she said to Po Chia, 'let us try first my plan. We shall set up a pavilion along the way our daughter must pass. We shall have music and singing, and we shall prepare a great feast. Surely she will see then that our way of life is the best.'

"All this was done. But the good maiden turned her head away saying, 'I prefer to go out to the World of Shadows.' So the angry Emperor gave the order that her head should be cut off. All the court assembled before the palace gate. The people looked on. The great ax was lifted. But the heavens grew dark and the ax broke into pieces as it touched the neck of Miao Shan. Again the Emperor of Heaven had heard her prayers. He sent the God of the Neighborhood in the form of a tiger to rescue the princess. Upon the back of the beast poor Miao Shan was carried away.

"The gentle maiden, who had fainted, opened her eyes in a strange place. All was dim and still. There were no plants or flowers. No sun, moon, or stars lighted the sky. No sound was heard. No hen cackled. No dog barked. Then a fine young man dressed in shining blue garments came forth to greet her.

" 'You have come to the underworld, Miao Shan,' he said. 'Here men are punished for the wrongs they have done upon the earth. The Emperor of Darkness has sent me to show you about through his realm. We have heard that your prayers drive away sadness. Can this be true? And will you say a prayer now so that we may hear it?'

"Miao Shan consented, on the condition that all the poor creatures who were being punished should be set free. She began to pray, and, my children, the darkness was lifted. Bright light filled the place, lilies covered the earth, and the dim underworld became a paradise of light and beauty.

"When she came back to earth, Miao Shan sought a quiet spot where she might think and pray and become good enough for the Heavenly Kingdom. As she wandered about she met an old man with a huge bulging forehead. In one hand he carried a stick of gnarled wood; in the other, a peach. It was Old Long Life himself, the god who can make a man live forever. Old Long Life greeted Miao Shan and put the peach into her hands.

" 'When you have eaten this peach, you will no longer feel hunger or thirst, and you will live forever,' he said.

"Again the God of the Neighborhood was commanded by the Emperor of Heaven to take the form of a tiger. Upon his back he carried Miao Shan safely on her long journey to a rocky island, called Pu To, that lies in the Southern Sea, where she found peace at last.

"For nine years there the maiden prayed. She thought only good thoughts, and at last she became perfect. Then one day spirits and gods assembled from all the corners of the earth. From the Eastern Mountain, from the Western Mountain, from the mountains of the North and the South, and from the mountain in the center of the world they came to honor Miao Shan. The Dragon Emperor of the Sea was there. The gods of the wind, the rain, and the thunder, the spirits of heaven and earth, all gathered to see her take her seat upon her golden throne, which was shaped like the lotus blossom.

"Then one day Miao Shan received a message from the Emperor of Heaven, telling her that she might now leave

For nine years Miao Shan thought only good thoughts and at last she became perfect

the earth and enter his kingdom. She was just about to set foot inside the shining gates of heaven when she looked back at the earth. She heard the cries of millions of poor people who were sad or in trouble, and she turned back to help them. From that time her name was changed from Miao Shan to Gwan Yin, which means 'She-Who-Hears-Prayers.'

"On her rocky island in the Southern Sea there is a tiny temple, so I have heard it told, called, 'The home of Gwan Yin, who would not go away.' It was built by a sailor whose life the goddess had saved. One day this sailor was out in his boat when he suddenly found it caught in a mass of lily blossoms that covered the sea like a carpet. So thickly they grew that he could not force his way through them. Like other wise seamen, this sailor had on his boat a statue of Gwan Yin. He kowtowed before this, saying, 'O gentle Gwan Yin, come to my aid! Open a way through these tangled lilies. If you would go with me to my own land, so be it. Or if you would that I go to your shores, show me the way.' A gentle breeze blew over the lilies. Their leaves rustled like silk as their blossoms closed tight. They sank beneath the clear water and a straight path was opened. The boatman followed its course which led to Gwan Yin's island of Pu To. There he built a little temple and put in it that statue of Gwan Yin which had saved his life."

Grandmother Ling often told the children stories of wonderful things that Gwan Yin had done. Everywhere through their land there were temples to this gentle goddess. Women brought her offerings of incense and paper money. They laid near her statues finely embroidered slippers and tiny dolls dressed like wee babies, in the hope that she would hear their prayers for children.

Ships came by the thousands every year to the island where Gwan Yin sat so long upon her lotus throne. Millions visited the temples built in honor of her. They prayed before her statues. They believed she would help them. The Chinese truly loved their gentle Goddess of Mercy.

The little prayer that Yu Lang whispered when she kowtowed to the gilt statue standing so calmly on the table in the family hall was that she might become beautiful. Sometimes her grandmother told the little girl that she was growing to look like Gwan Yin. This always filled Yu Lang with delight, for she knew that this goddess was the most beautiful as well as the most perfect woman who had ever lived.

As Grandmother Ling finished her story and rose from the table she made a last kowtow to the gilded statue. "Lady of Great Mercy and Great Pity," she prayed as her body swayed back and forth, "save us from sadness, save us from harm!" And the family went their ways with happiness and peace in their hearts.

V

THE GOD THAT LIVED IN THE KITCHEN

"Little pig!"

"Greedy ox!"

The angry voices of the children rang loud across the courtyard. They did not often quarrel, and their cross tones sounded strange inside the peaceful gray walls that shut in the Ling homestead.

Old Wang Lai, their nurse, came hurrying out of their

low house to see what the matter could be. At the same moment Huang Ying opened the door of the Old Old One's apartment.

"Old Mistress says Ah Shung and Yu Lang must come into her room," Huang Ying called out. The boy and the girl stopped their quarrel at once. As they crossed the veranda and entered their grandmother's room they looked sullenly at each other as if to say, "It was your fault."

"Sit down on that stool, Ah Shung, and you sit there, Yu Lang," the old woman said sternly as she laid her embroidery down on the bed where she was sitting. The day was cold, and she found its heated bricks the most comfortable seat.

"Now tell me what caused you to throw stones of unkindness into our calm stream of happiness?" she commanded, fixing her sharp black eyes upon the children.

"Ah Shung wanted my candied apricot, Lao Lao," Yu Lang began, hanging her head.

"She had more than she could eat, O Honorable Grandmother," Ah Shung said, shifting about on his stool.

"He pulled my hair," the little girl sobbed, and she held out the red cord with which her braid had been wound.

"She pulled my queue too," the boy said uneasily.

"Naughty children! You act like the dogs that slink through the streets and snarl at each other. Four horses cannot bring back cross words once they are spoken. Have you forgotten the God that lives in the Kitchen? This very night he flies up to heaven to make his report to the

Emperor there. What tales he will tell about your behavior!"

The children looked frightened. They had indeed forgotten the Kitchen God whose picture hung in a nook up over the brick stove upon which the family cooking was done. They knew well that he watched everything that went on inside the red gate, in order to report to the Emperor of the Gods when he made his annual visit to heaven at this time of the Small New Year.

"I will tell you the story of the God of the Kitchen once more," said old Grandmother Ling. "Then perhaps you will not forget so quickly again. It was long, long ago that there lived in our land a very old man whose name was Chang Kung. Inside his family walls there dwelt his sons and his grandsons, his great-grandsons and their great-great-grandsons. So many people were there and so many houses that it was like a small city.

"But even with the hundreds of people living there together, all was quiet and peaceful. Never a quarrel was known. Never were there heard in the Chang courts cross voices such as those which we heard here today. Everyone was contented. The one hundred dogs that lived inside the Chang walls never ceased wagging their tails. Indeed, it is said that these dogs were so kind to each other that they would wait to begin eating if one of them was late for his dinner.

"The fame of this household spread as far and as wide over the land as the breezes blow in the springtime. And at last it reached the ears of the Emperor himself upon his Dragon Throne.

"Now it so happened that the Emperor was about to make his yearly journey to the great Eastern Mountain in order to send his prayers up to heaven from its high peak. So, having heard of Chang Kung, he decided to visit his remarkable household upon his way back.

"What a sight that must have been! The procession began with the Emperor's guards. Tall men they were, the tallest in all the land and also the bravest. In their costumes of blue and red, with their long bows and arrows, they looked fine indeed. Then came the mandarins, important men who belonged to the Emperor's court, with their gowns embroidered with golden birds and beasts, and with blue and green peacock feathers in their round hats. In the army of attendants that marched with the Emperor there were men to carry the huge red umbrellas, men to play music, and even cooks to prepare feasts for the imperial stomach.

"The Emperor came last, riding in a sedan chair whose curtains and sides of bright yellow silk were embroidered with dragons. The sturdy men who carried his imperial chair on their shoulders were clad in suits of red cloth. Never before had such visitors entered the gates of the Changs.

"The aged Chang Kung met his imperial guest upon his knees. He kowtowed before him and greeted him with polite words of welcome.

" 'Very Excellent and Very Aged Sir,' said the Emperor, 'it is said that inside your walls no cross word has ever been spoken. Can that be true?'

" 'Lord of Ten Thousand Years,' Chang Kung replied humbly, 'you do my poor house far too much honor. It is true that the unworthy members of my family do not quarrel. Soft words please the gods, and we are content here. It would bring blessings upon our roofs, Shining One, if you would consent to walk through our courts and judge for yourself!'

"So the Emperor made his way through the gates that led from one court into the other. He looked into the houses and questioned the people. He found that they lived together like those lovebirds to each of which the gods gave only one eye and only one wing so that they might fly in pairs, breast to breast, helping each other.

"In the great Chang Hall of Politeness the Emperor was served with food and drink to refresh him. As he sipped the pale tea from cups as thin as fine paper, he said to his host, 'Excellent One of Great Age, my messengers spoke truly. I find no ripple of discontent upon your sea of happiness. Even the dogs here are polite to one another. You must have discovered some golden secret in order to keep so many people living together in such order and peace. I should like to know that secret myself.'

"Old Chang Kung called to his servants to bring forth the four precious gems of the library. They set forth on a table a tablet of smooth split bamboo, for in those days people did not know about paper, my children. Beside it they laid out the rabbit-hair brush, the ink stick and the ink stone with its small well of water. Chang Kung wet the black ink stick and rubbed its soft end on the flat stone. He dipped his brush into the ink paste. With delicate strokes he began to brush words on the tablet. One hundred words he wrote. Then with a low bow he placed the tablet in the hands of the curious Emperor.

" 'You have written many words, but at the same time you have written only one word,' the Emperor exclaimed in surprise.

" 'Ai, but that one word is the golden secret, O Son of Heaven,' Chang Kung said, slowly nodding his gray head up and down.

"What was the one word, Lao Lao?" Ah Shung asked as his grandmother paused.

"The word he had written one hundred times, my children, was 'kindness.'

"The Emperor was so pleased that he himself took up the brush and wrote. Upon a large tablet he set down his joy in finding such a household as that of Chang Kung's. He gave permission to have his words pasted upon the great gate, where everyone who came in or who went out might see them.

"You may be sure that the fame of Chang Kung grew even greater. People asked for his picture so that peace and happiness might rule in their homes as in his. It would be well, my naughty ones, if you should go to our kitchen.

Get down on your knees. Make your kowtows toward the picture of Chang Kung up over the stove. Beg him to forget the cross words you have spoken."

The two children went with their nurse, old Wang Lai, to do as their grandmother bade them. The picture of the Kitchen God in his nook over the stove was smeared with smoke from the cooking fires. But the boy and girl looked up with respect at the old man in his red-and-blue robes. In this picture several children with smiling faces were shown gathered about him.

Ah Shung and Yu Lang always enjoyed the evening of the twenty-third of the Twelfth Moon when the Kitchen God flew away to spend seven days in the Heavenly Kingdom. The Old Old One herself entered the kitchen as evening came on. She set out with her own hands the steamed cakes and the wine and the other things that were to honor the messenger of heaven. Lao Lao's oldest son took the picture of the Kitchen God from its tiny palace over the stove. Then Grandmother Ling smeared the mouth of the picture with a sweet, sticky sirup.

"He will lick his lips," she said to the children. "He will taste the sweet sirup and surely he will remember only good things about us when he makes his report to the Emperor of the Sky."

A little sedan chair made of bamboo and paper was waiting to receive the picture of the Kitchen God. The whole Ling family followed as this was carried into the Courtyard of Politeness, where honored guests were received. There a bonfire had been made, and it crackled as the flames licked the edges of the dry straw.

Everyone bowed low as the picture of the Kitchen God in its paper chair was put on the center of the fire. As the gray smoke floated upward on the frosty air, the Lings were sure that the Kitchen God was mounting to the sky. They burned a paper horse for him to ride upon, and they poured cups of tea and wine on the ashes so that he should not be thirsty during his journey.

Ah Shung and his boy cousins were allowed to set off the red firecrackers which so please the gods. With glowing sticks of incense they lighted one after another. The popping filled the children with delight, for to them the sound of firecrackers always meant fun and feasting. For the Lings every important holiday began with the noise of bursting firecrackers. They believed that good spirits loved their din, but that bad spirits were frightened. Thus, the more firecrackers you set off, the safer you were.

In Grandmother Ling's apartment that evening the family feasted on the steamed cakes which had been made in honor of the Kitchen God's going away. Candied fruit and melon seeds were passed round, and the room was filled with chatter and laughter. The Old Old One seemed to have quite forgotten the unseemly behavior of Ah Shung and Yu Lang. As the children munched their sugared fruit they hoped very much that the Kitchen God, too, had forgotten their fault.

VI

GUARDIANS OF THE GATE

Cʜᴀɴɢ is pasting the gods on the gate," Ah Shung called to his sister, Yu Lang, as he peeped around the spirit wall that shielded the Moon Gate in the Court of Politeness.

It was the day just before the New Year, the merriest of all the holidays in the Chinese calendar. In the Ling courtyards people were going and coming, everyone bent on some important errand. Ah Shung ran through the Moon Gate and into the entrance court. Yu Lang followed, but she went more slowly because of her poor little bound feet. Behind the two children came their old nurse, Wang Lai. She was as eager as they to see what was going on at the red gate that led in from the city.

"How splendid the gate looks!" Yu Lang exclaimed. The great entrance gleamed in the winter sunlight. It looked glossier and redder than ever for it had lately been given a new coat of a special red varnish called lacquer. Over the gate, facing the world outside, was a long sign made of peach wood, also lacquered red. Upon it were some raised golden symbols which were the Chinese word pictures for "Good Luck to This Household."

"We are ready for the New Year," Old Chang, the gate-keeper, said, wagging his gray head and admiring the gate. The Chinese have always loved red. To them it is the color of joy and good luck. Over every door that opened upon the entrance court were red papers with lucky words cut out of them. Even the gates to the stables and the jinrikisha sheds had New Year trimmings of red. This first day of the First Moon was thought to be the very best day for luck in the whole year.

Old Chang was pressing flat a gaily colored picture which he had just pasted on one of the red doors of the gate. This picture showed an ancient warrior with a frowning black face. On the other half of the gate there was already pasted the likeness of another warrior whose face was white. With their eyes staring, and with their bows and arrows in hand, surely these gods of the gate were fierce enough to frighten any bad spirits that might come their way. Ah Shung and Yu Lang, Old Chang and Wang Lai, and, indeed, every man, woman, and child inside the Ling walls firmly believed that these gods kept bad spirits away from the gate.

When the boy and his sister went again to the family court they met their grandmother and Huang Ying coming back from the kitchen. The Old Mistress had been visiting the cooks to be sure that the New Year cakes and the meat dumplings, the New Year porridge, and all the other good things were ready for the feasting that would begin on the morrow and last through the month.

"Bring tea, Huang Ying," the old woman said to her maid. "Ah Shung will help me into my room. Let there be tea bowls for three."

While the two children sipped the hot tea from thin blue-and-white bowls they told their grandmother of their visit to Chang and the red gate.

"It is well," the Old Old One said, nodding her head when they spoke of the gate gods. "When our red gate is shut tight we shall seal its cracks with paper. Then nothing can come in to spoil our New Year luck."

"Who are those fierce men on the gate-pictures, Lao Lao?" Yu Lang asked between sips of tea and bites of steamed cakes.

"Perhaps they are Shen Shu and Yu Lu," the old woman explained. "I will tell you the story about them.

"As I heard my grandmother say," she began, "in the very earliest times there was a mountain in the Eastern

Ocean upon which there grew a great peach tree. It was not at all like the peach trees in our Garden of Sweet Smells. Its trunk was larger around than the walls of our city. Its branches grew so long that it would take Wong, the jinrikisha man, many years to trot along the edge of the shadow they made on the earth.

"Now some of the lowest branches of this tree grew toward the northeast. They leaned toward each other, forming an arch, and through this there flew in and out of the world all the spirits of the air and the earth and the water.

"Two good spirits, whose names were Shen Shu and Yu Lu, were chosen by the Emperor of Heaven to stand guard over this gate that led in and out of the world. Ai, they were clever, those gate guards, Shen Shu and Yu Lu. They could tell at a glance which spirits were good and which spirits were bad.

"As soon as the gate guards saw a bad spirit they tied it up tight and threw it to the tigers. The Emperor who then sat upon the Dragon Throne of our Flowery Kingdom heard of these clever gate guards. He thought he should like them to protect his own palace doors. So he called for the court artists.

" 'Take tablets of lucky peach wood,' he commanded. 'Paint upon them the likenesses of the guardians of the gates on the Eastern Mountain. Give them bows and arrows and spears. Then hang them upon the gates where the spirits can see them. Shen Shu and Yu Lu know bad spirits from good spirits. They will allow only the good spirits to come into my palace.' "

"Are those men that Chang, the gatekeeper, has pasted on our doors really Shen Shu and Yu Lu, Lao Lao?" Ah Shung asked, his black eyes shining bright with wonder at his grandmother's tale.

"O-yo, Little Bear, that I do not know," the old woman replied. "There are other guardians of the gate and another tale about them. Perhaps these are the ones that are protecting our sky-wells. Long, long ago there was in our land an Emperor whose name was Shih Ming. One day he fell ill. He could not sleep at night because bad spirits disturbed him. They threw tiles down from the roof. They hurled bricks at his door. They hooted and howled. All the night through they made such a clatter and din that Shih Ming could not rest.

"In the morning the Emperor was ill indeed. Doctors from the four corners of the empire gathered around him. The minsters of the court were called together.

" 'This True Dragon is near death,' the doctors declared. 'His blood runs too hot. His mind is troubled with strange ideas. He hears nothing by day, but at night the spirits torment him. We do not know what to do.'

"Then there came forward a brave general whose name was Chin Shu-pao. He fell on his knees and kowtowed to the sick Emperor. 'Shining Son of Heaven,' he said, knocking his head on the ground, 'this unworthy servant of yours may be able to help you. He has killed men as easily

as he cuts open a gourd. In battle the dead bodies left
behind him are like ants in a hill. Why should he fear
spirits? Why should his brave comrade, Hu Ching-te, be
afraid? Let us both arm ourselves and let us stand
by your door through the night to drive the spirits
away.'

"Chin and Hu took up their posts beside the palace
door. All night they stood on guard, and not once was
there a sound to disturb the sick Emperor. He slept the
night through, and from that moment his illness began
to grow less. Night after night Chin and Hu stood by the
door, until at last the Emperor recovered. But although
he was well again he still feared that the spirits might
come back if no guard stood on watch. At the same time
he was troubled about his faithful Chin Shu-pao and
Hu Ching-te.

" 'The good generals must be weary,' Shih Ming said
to his ministers. 'They need to rest. Call the court paint-
ers! Bid them paint likenesses of the brave Chin and Hu.
Let the artists show them with armor and weapons so that
they may be ready for the spirits! Then paste their pictures on the gates of the palace. We shall see if they will
not be as powerful against the bad spirits as Chin and
Hu themselves.'

"It was done. The pictures were fixed upon the gates
of the palace. Ha, the spirits must have thought the
painted figures were really the mighty warriors themselves,
for none came that night to disturb the peace inside the

palace walls." Grandmother Ling laughed as she thought of the good joke on the spirits who were so stupid as to be so easily fooled.

The Ling family took every care to start the New Year with good luck. Besides the lucky red signs and the lucky dishes being prepared inside the family kitchen, they did not forget a single lucky custom. They were more than usually polite as they put up over the stove the new picture of the Kitchen God who, they thought, had returned from his visit to heaven. Knives and scissors and sharp tools were all put carefully away lest the New Year luck should be cut.

Throughout the evening the courtyards were filled with the din of popping firecrackers. Ah Shung and Yu Lang were allowed to light some of the little red tubes of gunpowder themselves. They enjoyed the sound of their bursting. The Chinese all liked their noise because they believed it helped to frighten the spirits away.

"It was in earliest times," the Old Old One had told the children, "that we found out that the bad spirits do not like sharp sounds. In the Western Mountain there was once a giant more than twice as tall as your father. He was so ugly to look upon that men fainted away when they saw him. At last they learned to drive him off by burning hollow stalks of bamboo, which made a crackling noise. Then someone or other thought of putting gunpowder inside hollow tubes made of paper. These first firecrackers made a much louder noise than burning bamboo.

They frightened the ugly giant so badly that he never came back again.

"Tomorrow morning we shall break the paper seals that Chang has pasted over the cracks of the gates, and we shall open our doors to fortune with lucky phrases. Every one of us must guard his tongue against saying the wrong words. You, my thoughtless small ones, must take special care what word you speak first when you wake in the morning. For if it is a lucky word, you will be lucky through all the New Year. But if it is unlucky, o-yo, there will be trouble."

The boy and the girl trotted off with Wang Lai across the dark court to their own low house. The cold winter sky was dotted with stars, and the sound of popping firecrackers still came over the walls from the courtyards of neighboring houses. Ah Shung and Yu Lang exchanged their wadded day suits for their night garments of softer cloth. They climbed up on the heated brick floor of their bed, they arranged their hard little pillows of leather and wood, and they rolled themselves in their thick wadded comforters with sighs of content. They were tired with the excitement of the day's preparations. They wanted to go to sleep quickly so that the New Year would come soon. They could hardly wait for the gifts and the good things that the Old Man of the New Year would bring to them.

As Wang Lai pulled the bed curtains that shut them away from the night air, they were saying over and over to themselves the word they meant to speak the first thing in the morning. They decided upon it because it was the very word for good luck. If they could just remember to say it first, they would be sure of a splendid New Year.

"Fu. Fu. Fu-u-u . . ." Yu Lang whispered sleepily.

"Fu. Fu. Fu-u-u-u . . ." Ah Shung echoed. And then all was still inside their bed curtains.

VII

THE PAINTED EYEBROW

Yu Lang was watching her grandmother dress. It was a day in the New Year holiday time, and there were to be important guests in the Court of Politeness. The old woman seemed to be taking more than ordinary care with her appearance, although Yu Lang could never remember a day when the Old Old One did not look as if she had stepped down from a scroll painting.

Lao Lao was sitting in her carved wooden chair before a little table. She had placed herself near the wide latticed windows which filled half of the south side of her room. She wanted to get as much as possible of the light coming through the thin white paper that served instead of glass in the window frames. Upon the table before her was a mahogany box whose open lid stood upright and whose body was filled with little boxes and bottles of powder and paint, with combs and brushes and jars of "hair water."

Grandmother Ling was gazing intently into the square mirror inside the lid of the mahogany box. She was watching her maid, Huang Ying, who was combing her gray hair with one ivory comb after another. Each of the seven combs the maid used was smaller than the one before, and when she had finished, the old woman's hair lay smooth as silk on her head. With a brush dipped into the hair water the maid went over it for one last time before she coiled it upon her Old Mistress' neck and thrust a gold dagger-shaped pin through the flat knot. The hair water was made of a kind of gum, so sticky that it kept every lock pasted tightly in place.

"Be sure your hand is steady now, Huang Ying," the old woman said when her maid began to draw a fine line of black above one of her eyes. Both of her eyebrows were bare. Every one of their hairs had been plucked out, like the feathers of the fowls that go into the cooking pots.

"Why does Huang Ying paint your face, Lao Lao?"

the little girl asked her grandmother as she gazed fascinated by the work of the maid.

"I do not put quite so much red on my lips and my cheeks as your mother and the younger women, Little Jade Flower," Grandmother Ling replied, "but because one has grown to an honorable age is no reason for offending the eyes of her neighbors with ugliness."

"But why do you not let your own eyebrows grow like mine?" Yu Lang persisted. "Then you would not have to have Huang Ying make you new ones each morning."

"Ai, Little Curious," the old woman said smiling, "that would indeed seem much simpler. But it is not the custom. Who started the fashion, I do not know. Perhaps it was Chen Lien and her ugly eyebrow."

"Oh, Lao Lao, who was she?" Yu Lang cried in delight, for she scented a story.

"Chen Lien was a maiden who lived in early times," her grandmother began. "She had a skin whiter than rice. Her waist was as slender as a skein of fine silk. Her eyes were the shape of the oval kernel of the almond. When she walked on her lily feet she swayed like a young bamboo. But her beauty was spoiled because she had only one perfect eyebrow. The other was cut through by a scar caused by an accident when she was small like you, Flower-child.

"One spring day, as Chen Lien sat in her garden, a young man climbed up a tall willow tree just outside the wall in order to free his kite which had become tangled up in its branches. From his perch high above the ground the young man, whom we might as well call Wu Fang, looked over the wall and caught sight of Chen Lien. The side of her face with the perfect eyebrow was turned toward him, and so fair did the maiden look there in the garden that the young man straightway fell in love with her. He went home to his parents and told them that at last he would consent to marry, as they had so long wished. But he told them also that he would have no other bride than the maiden who sat in the garden beside the tall willow tree.

"The parents of Wu Fang sent for a go-between, a man who was known to be very successful in making arrangements for families with sons and daughters of the age to be married. They consulted the fortune tellers to find out whether the wedding of Chen Lien and Wu Fang would bring good luck to the young people and both their households.

" 'It is best I should tell you something, O Excellent Youth,' the go-between said to Wu Fang. 'The young maiden is good. The young maiden is rich. The young maiden is fair. But still you should know that there is a flaw in her beauty.'

"But Wu Fang would not listen. 'I myself have a way of knowing that the young maiden's appearance is all I could desire,' he said. 'If there is a slight flaw, that is nothing to me. I will marry Chen Lien.' He did not wish to explain that he had looked over the wall and had seen the

So fair did the maiden look there in the garden that the young man straightway fell in love with her

maiden himself, because he well knew that he had broken the rules of good behavior.

"The girl's parents were delighted with the marriage plan, for the family of Wu Fang was one of the best in the neighborhood. Also, they had secretly feared that her ugly eyebrow might prevent their daughter from making a really good match.

"Well, in due time there arrived at the bride's gate a card from the groom, giving the date of the wedding which the fortune tellers advised, and, as is the custom, there came along with it a pair of handsome fat geese whose sad white feathers had been covered with a coat of joyous red paint. The bride's family politely returned one of the geese with their consent to the date which the groom had selected.

"As the day itself drew near, the courtyard of Chen Lien's home was heaped high with presents from the groom's family. There were earrings and finger rings, bracelets and hair ornaments, rolls of fine silk, and sweet candies and cakes in handsome boxes of red lacquer.

"But Chen Lien was troubled. 'Oh, what will my bridegroom say when he sees my ugly eyebrow?' she cried to her mother.

" 'No doubt the go-between has already told him, my daughter. Think no more about it,' her mother said, comforting her. But through all the preparations for the wedding, even during the painful moments when the maids were pulling out the hairs in her girlish bangs so that her forehead should be high and smooth like a wife's, the poor maiden could not put the thought of her eyebrow out of her mind.

"Now, time never stands still, little Yu Lang." Grandmother Ling continued her tale. "The wedding day drew near. Gifts from the bride's family and the bride's own belongings arrived at the Wu gate at last. All the neighborhood gathered to see the bundles and boxes. Each red lacquered table, borne by two porters, was so heavily loaded that the men had to walk slowly.

"Next day, dressed in her bridal robe of red silk with golden patterns embroidered upon it, Chen Lien set forth in her marriage chair. Its curtains of red cloth were closed tight to shut her away from the eyes of the world. Firecrackers were set off to speed her on her way. She wept, as all good brides do, so that her family should not think she was glad to be leaving them.

"But Chen Lien wept more than is necessary for any bride. She was not even cheered by the thought of the splendid procession that accompanied her. Through cracks in the curtains she could see the two lines of men dressed in red, carrying the flying red banners, the huge red umbrellas, the lanterns, and the great golden symbols high up on poles. The sound of the music of the trumpets and horns could not drive from her mind the fear of what her new husband should say when he saw the ugly scar on her brow, where the hair would not grow.

"In this wedding all was done according to custom. The

bridegroom in his scarlet robe and black over-vest came
forth to meet the procession. When for the first time
Chen Lien saw how handsome he was, she felt even sadder
than before to think that her own beauty was spoiled.
Firecrackers popped as her chair was carried into the
entrance court. Wu Fang, the bridegroom, shot three dull-
pointed arrows at the floor of the sedan chair so as to drive
away any spirits which might bring bad luck. Chen Lien
was glad that the thick veil of beads hanging from her
gilt marriage crown covered her face. She bent her head
modestly as the women from Wu Fang's family led her
into the house.

"The ceremonies were over all too quickly for Chen
Lien. She and her bridegroom met in the great Hall of
the Ancestors. She dutifully knelt down on the floor beside
her new husband and kowtowed to the Gods of Heaven
and Earth. They bowed to the ancestors and they bowed
to each other. Later they bowed to the guests and the
parents. Then they drank the marriage wine from two
cups tied together with the red cord of joy, and they ate
the wedding rice.

"So they were married. At last the feasting was over.
The moment arrived when Chen Lien must raise her bead
veil so that her husband might have his first look at her
face. Of course, Little Flower, it is never good to show
dismay, but who could blame the young bridegroom for
starting when he saw Chen Lien's ugly eyebrow?

" 'O Excellent Sir,' Chen Lien said, with tears in her

eyes as she noticed the surprised look on his face, 'did not the go-between tell you about my poor ugly eyebrow? It happened when I was a child. With my honorable parents I was visiting in the courts of distant friends. As we played in the garden there, a small boy threw a stone. I am sure that he did not intend it should hit me, but it struck me full on the brow and it cut a deep gash. When the wound was healed it left this scar which, alas, will remain with me until I go to the World of Shadows.'

" 'What was the name of that small boy, O Lady of Unsurpassed Sweetness?' Wu Fang asked his bride gently.

" 'Noble youth,' she replied, 'I do not know. He was a guest like myself, making a visit.'

" 'Were the courts in which you were playing those of the Li family in the City of Pleasant Rest?' he asked with a note of excitement in his low voice.

" 'How could you know that, O Excellent Husband?' Chen Lien cried in surprise.

" 'Because that boy was myself,' Wu Fang exclaimed, quite forgetting to be calm in his astonishment at the strange ways of heaven. 'My parents have often told me the story of the poor little girl whose brow was cut open by the stone I threw across the Li garden. The gods themselves must have arranged that our ankles should be joined with the red cord of marriage in order that I might repair the damage I did so many years ago. And they have put into my mind just what I must do.'

"Wu Fang called for black paint and his rabbit-hair

writing brush. He dipped the brush in the black paste, and with careful strokes he painted a new eyebrow upon Chen Lien's scar. He made it just the shape of a young willow leaf. Thin and curved, it was so like her perfect eyebrow that none could tell one from the other.

"And every morning thereafter, my little Yu Lang, throughout all the happy years that Chen Lien dwelt in the Wu courtyards, her loving husband, Wu Fang, painted a new willow-leaf eyebrow upon that scar which he had caused. So did the gods bring joy out of sadness. And so perhaps did the women of China learn that the hand of man may sometimes improve on the handiwork of the gods."

VIII

TING LAN AND THE LAMB

Leaning on the arm of her maid, Huang Ying, the Old Old One led the way across the courtyards and through the gate to the Hall of the Ancestors. Behind her walked the younger women of the family, carrying bowls of rice and pots of tea and wine. Last of all came Ah Shung and Yu Lang and the other children.

"Our honorable guests from on high must be well cared for during their visit under our roofs," the old woman reminded the family every morning during the weeks of the New Year holidays. At the beginning of this festival time the Lings believed that the spirits of their forefathers floated down from the Heavenly Kingdom like spring blossoms on the breeze. They took great pains to welcome them

66

to all the family feasts. They showed them the greatest respect in order that they might be pleased and so bring the household good luck.

In the great Hall of the Ancestors, facing the door, there was a high narrow table set against the wall, almost like a mantel shelf. Upon its shining black top there stood a number of narrow wood tablets about twelve inches tall. These little tablets were lacquered bright red. Each one had upon it a raised gold word picture that stood for the name of one of the Ling ancestors. In this land of Ah Shung and Yu Lang people do not use an alphabet. Their writing is not at all like that in America. Each Chinese word has its own sign or picture.

For the New Year feast for the forefathers the Old Old One had placed a square table on which eight places were laid and about which eight chairs were set. The old woman lighted the candles upon the high table and set fire to sticks of incense, in a little bronze urn, that sweetened the air with their scented smoke. Politely she held the incense burner in her two hands and raised it as high as her bent head, as though she were offering it to her spirit guests. Then she set it down before the red-and-gold tablets.

In the same way Lao Lao offered each of the eight cups of wine, which she poured from a porcelain pot that Huang Ying had brought her, and each of the eight rice bowls, which she set on the square table with her own hands.

As head of the family, Grandmother Ling was the first

to kneel on the floor before the honorable ancestors. She kowtowed three times. Then she rose and took her place at the side of the room, while each member of the family in turn made his low bows. Back and forth! Back and forth! Back and forth! As they knelt before the red-and-gold tablets Ah Shung and Yu Lang bent their small bodies until their foreheads almost touched the gray tiles of the floor.

For about ten minutes the Lings all stood in a row at the side of the room, silent in order that the forefathers might not be disturbed as they partook of the feast. Then Grandmother Ling lifted a cup of hot tea and offered it to the ancestors. Then slowly she pushed back its saucer-like cover and let three drops of the tea fall on the ground. In the same way she poured out three drops of wine. These were offerings for the gods, whom the Lings always wished to please.

Ah Shung and Yu Lang enjoyed the New Year feasts of the ancestors, but in secret they told each other that the part they liked best was when the farewell kowtows had been made and the forefathers' rice had been reheated and served at their own table in the family hall.

"Whenever I go into the Hall of the Ancestors and see their honorable tablets, I remember Ting Lan and the lamb," Grandmother Ling said, while she was resting for a few moments before starting back toward the family hall. "Stand close to my chair, my small ones, and I will tell you about them.

"This tale of Ting Lan and the lamb comes from the ancient great teacher, Confucius. So it is well worth remembering. It happened, in times long gone by, that there lived a youth named Ting Lan. O-yo, he was a worthless fellow. A wicked young man and cruel, too, he was. He often beat his old mother so hard that her cries could be heard all through his village. In every way he could think of he made her life miserable. She had fed him and clothed him and cared for him tenderly when he was a child. But Ting Lan, it seemed, never thought of all that.

"One day the cruel young man was tending his flock of sheep out on a hillside beside a swift river. As he watched them, he noticed a hungry lamb go to its mother. He saw the little white creature kneel humbly at the side of the ewe in order to drink the milk from her bag.

" 'How sweetly that little lamb kneels to its mother! And how different is the treatment my poor mother receives!' Ting Lan thought to himself. And as he sat there on the grass, watching the lamb, the youth was suddenly ashamed. 'From this moment I shall be different,' he declared. 'I shall remember this lamb. I, too, shall be gentle. All the rest of my life I shall try to make up to my mother for my wicked treatment of her.'

"Just then the old woman herself came over the hill. When he saw her the youth jumped to his feet and started toward her.

" 'I shall kneel to my good mother now,' he decided. 'I shall tell her how ashamed I am of my past behavior.

I shall ask her to forgive me. And I shall promise to be
a dutiful son in the future.'

"But his mother could not see inside her son's mind.
She could not know that the cruel youth had changed his
ways. She thought he was running toward her in order
to beat her, and she was afraid that she would soon feel
the staff he held in his hand upon her old back. So she,
too, began to run. She sped down the hillside and jumped
into the swirling water of the swift river.

"Ting Lan was filled with sorrow and dismay. He
jumped in after his mother and swam about, trying to
find her. He searched and he searched but with no success.
She had disappeared. No doubt the good dragon who lived
in the river had received her as his guest.

"But on the top of the water, at the exact spot where
his mother had jumped in from the riverbank, there
floated a small piece of flat wood, oblong in shape.

" 'I shall take home this bit of wood to remind me of my
poor mother,' Ting Lan said to himself. He carved her
name upon the wood tablet and he set it in the place of
greatest honor inside his house. He never forgot to kowtow nor to set out bowls of food and wine before it at each
festival time. The spirit of Ting Lan's mother must have
been pleased, for good luck followed the youth all through
his life.

"People say that the piece of wood which Ting Lan
took from the stream was the very first tablet to an ancestor. They think it was about the same shape and size of
those on our table here."

The children looked at the red-and-gold tablets with even more respect and interest when their grandmother told them that the spirits of their grandfather and their great-grandparents really dwelt beside the oblong pieces of wood.

"When I myself go to the World of Shadows," the Old Old One explained, rising from her chair, "my spirit will divide itself into three parts. One part will go to be a guest of the Heavenly Emperor. One part will remain with my body under a heap of earth out among the shady grave mounds in the midst of our family fields. The third part will often come to rest beside the little red tablet which will have my name upon it and which will be placed here in the Hall of the Ancestors.

"Remember the story of Ting Lan and the lamb, my children," Lao Lao said as she made her way to the door leaning up on Huang Ying's arm. "Obey your parents if you would keep sadness away from your doors. Act toward them as gently as Ting Lan's little lamb. And do not forget to do them honor when they have become guests on high and when their spirits, too, have joined the ancestors here."

IX

THE DAUGHTER OF THE DRAGON KING

How was it with Scholar Shih in the hall of learning today, Ah Shung?" asked Grandmother Ling one winter afternoon as she sat with her grandchildren gathered about her.

"It was good, Lao Lao," the boy answered. "Scholar Shih was graciously pleased with me. With my back turned so that I could not get help from his face, I could repeat without stopping four whole pages of the sayings of our wise teacher, Confucius. I have brought you some of the words I made with my writing brush."

The boy unrolled a strip of thin paper upon which he had painted a column of large word symbols, one below the other. Each stroke and dot was carefully done. Yu Lang looked at them admiringly. The little girl thought her brother's words looked as beautiful as the writing in the scroll poems that hung on the walls of the family hall. Indeed, all the younger children looked up to Ah Shung because he was learning to read and to write.

"You have done well, Little Bear," Grandmother Ling said, nodding her head in approval. "Your words are well made." The old woman was a beautiful writer herself. When she wrote she took as great care with each brush stroke as when she painted delicate pictures on strips of thin silk. Much pleased with her grandson, she rose from her chair and crossed the room to a red lacquer cabinet. From one of its many small drawers she took out a folded piece of soft yellow silk.

"This is for the young scholar, a reward for good work," she said, and she put the silk into the boy's hands. The other children gathered about him as he unfolded it. It was a triangle of yellow with a gorgeous green dragon twisting its snaky body about on it and trying to grasp a pearl with its curving claws.

"Our flag!" Ah Shung exclaimed in delight. "I shall hang it over our brick bed, Yu Lang. It will be good to have this dragon there to protect us from the bad spirits."

These Chinese children loved dragons. They believed

that these fairy-tale creatures really lived down under the waters, back in the mountains, and up in the sky. Just because they had never met a live dragon did not prove to Ah Shung and Yu Lang that they did not exist. They had seen dragons embroidered on satins and silks. Dragons were carved on the tables and chairs in the Hall of the Ancestors, and even on the bed frame in the Old Old One's room. Dragons on pictures, dragons painted on china, and dragons in their grandmother's stories made these flying serpents real to them.

Ah Shung and Yu Lang knew that dragons fighting in the sky made the thunder and shook the rain out of the clouds. Dragons brought good luck and kept unfriendly spirits away. The Emperor himself had chosen the dragon as his own special sign. The dragon was the national animal of all the land, and no one in the Flowery Kingdom doubted its goodness or power.

"Tell us a story about a dragon, Lao Lao," Yu Lang asked her grandmother, as Ah Shung laid his dragon flag across the side of a small table where everyone could admire it.

"Let me think," the old woman said, smiling. "Well then, I will tell you the tale of the Dragon King's daughter and how she rewarded the youth named Liu Ye.

"In a certain part of our land there was long, long ago a family named Liu. Their son, Liu Ye, had studied and studied to prepare for the examinations that were held every year by order of the Emperor. He hoped, when he had passed them, to receive a government position that would bring him much money.

"But, my children, in spite of the days and nights which poor Liu Ye spent in the examination cell, he did not pass. Take warning from him, Ah Shung! When you go to take the examinations yourself, be sure that you have studied enough and that you know your books by heart. This young man turned his face sadly toward home, and as he walked over the land he came upon a young woman who was tending her goats on the banks of the River Ching.

"Now this young woman was poorly dressed, but her face was as fair as a plum blossom in spring, and her body was as slender as a willow branch. Liu Ye was so struck by her beauty that he halted to speak to her.

" 'Good maiden,' he said, bowing politely, 'who may you be, and where do you come from?'

" 'O Excellent Sir,' the young woman replied, 'I am the youngest daughter of the Dragon King who lives in the Lake of Tung Ting. Not long ago my father gave me in marriage to the son of the dragon who lives in this river. His servants were jealous when I entered his palace. They told lies about me and my husband believed them. He put me outside his courts. I am now forced to earn my rice by tending the goats of the farmers in yonder village.' Tears rolled down the pale cheeks of the fair young woman, and the heart of Liu Ye was touched by her misery.

" 'What can I do to help you, O Daughter of the Dragon King?' he asked.

" 'Should you be going in the direction of the Lake of Tung Ting, you could indeed be of use to me, O Noble Young Man,' the weeping girl said.

" 'My home lies in that direction. You have but to command me,' Liu Ye replied with a bow.

" 'I would ever be grateful if you would deliver this letter to my father,' the young woman said. 'On the northern bank of the Lake of Tung Ting there stands a giant orange tree. Strike it thrice with your belt and there will come a messenger to guide you to the Dragon King's palace.'

" 'Liu Ye took the letter. As soon as he had returned to his home, he set forth across the fields until he came to the orange tree of which the young woman had told him. He unfastened his belt, and three times he lashed the trunk of the orange tree. At once there rose from the lake a young man dressed in armor and carrying a shining sword in his hand.

" 'Who struck yonder orange tree? Was it you, young man?' he said to Liu Ye.

" 'It was I,' Liu replied, 'I bear a message for the Dragon King who lives in the Lake of Tung Ting. I would go to his palace.'

"The young man in armor thrust his sword into the lake. The waters parted and he led Liu Ye safely to the palace of the Dragon King. What splendid sights the young man saw there! The Dragon King's palace was made of bright-colored stones, so clear that one could see through them almost as easily as through a hole in a window paper. Liu was led through one crystal door after another. He passed heaps of opals and pearls and he saw precious stones of beautiful colors.

"At last in one splendid courtyard he came upon the great Dragon King himself. He had the form of a man, dressed in robes of bright purple, and in his hand gleamed a piece of the purest green jade-stone.

" 'I come from your daughter, O Dragon King,' Liu Ye said, kowtowing before him. 'I live in the neighboring kingdom of Wu. I have spent years in study, and I was returning from the Examination Halls, where, alas, I failed to pass. As I was walking along I saw your fair daughter, tending her goats upon the banks of the River Ching. Her clothes were in tatters. Her shoes were worn through. She seemed so very sad that my heart wept at the sight. She gave me this letter to deliver to your majesty.'

"When the Dragon King read the pitiful letter from his beloved daughter, the tears flowed from his eyes. His attendants who stood near him began to weep and to wail.

" 'Stop that noise!' cried the Dragon King. 'Stop it at once! Chien Tang will hear.

" 'Who is Chien Tang?' asked Liu Ye.

" 'He is my elder brother,' the Dragon King answered. 'He is the dragon who once lived in the River Chien Tang. Now he is the king of all river dragons.'

" 'But why do you fear lest Chien Tang should hear the news I have brought you?'

" 'Ai, Chien Tang has a temper, a terrible temper,' the Dragon King said, shaking his head. 'Once, in years gone by, he flew into a rage and ordered his river dragons to send water flowing out over their banks. The flood he caused then covered the land with water deep as the ocean, and it lasted nine years.'

"The Dragon King had scarcely uttered the last word when there arose a clattering sound. A red dragon so large that it darkened the sky flew through the air. Its scales were red gold, its mane shone like fire, and its eyes flashed like lightning. Quicker than I can tell you, the giant red dragon disappeared into the clouds.

"The Dragon King barely had time to tell Liu Ye that the giant red dragon was his brother, Chien Tang, before the shining beast appeared once again. A lovely young woman rode on his back as he flew down from the heavens.

" 'It is the young woman who tended the goats!' Liu exclaimed in surprise.

" 'It is my dear youngest daughter,' the Dragon King cried.

" 'Ai, I found her in a sad plight,' the Red Dragon said, 'but I have punished her wicked husband. I have carried him off to my own kingdom. He will cause her sorrow no more.'

"The beautiful daughter of the Dragon King was so grateful to Liu Ye that she persuaded her father to offer her hand to him in marriage. But the young man was troubled. 'They have just killed her first husband,' he said to himself, 'I had best go on my way.' And so he refused.

" 'I only wished to reward you, O Excellent Youth,' the Dragon King's daughter said as she bade Liu Ye good-by. 'But perhaps the lucky hour has not yet arrived. We shall wait a while.'

"The youth went to his home. In time his family arranged a marriage for him with a daughter of the Chang family. But scarcely had they eaten the wedding rice when the bride died. Liu Ye's second marriage with a daughter of a family named Han was no more successful, for again the bride flew away to the Shadowy World.

" 'The gods do not smile upon me,' Liu Ye said to his mother. 'I shall go to another city to live. Perhaps there I shall find better luck.'

"But in the strange city the young man was lonely. 'I will take another wife,' he decided, and he went to seek a go-between to arrange matters for him.

" 'I know of a beautiful young widow.' the go-between said. 'Her husband has died, and since she is so young her mother is anxious that she should marry again.'

"Well, it all ended in Liu Ye's marrying the young widow. For more than a year they lived happily together, and when the gods sent them a son, the woman said to her husband, 'This blessing from heaven binds us together forever. Now I can tell you that I am the daughter of the Dragon King of Lake Tung Ting, the woman you saved from her misery on the banks of the River Ching. I made a vow I would reward you. I wished to marry you then, but you refused. My father forced me to wed the son of a silk merchant, but I never stopped wishing that the day might come when I should be your wife.'

"The story goes that Liu Ye and the Dragon King's daughter went to live in a splendid palace in the Lake of Tung Ting and that in time the fortunate youth became a dragon himself. In the books his name is written as 'Golden Dragon Great Prince.'"

X

THE BIG FEET OF THE EMPRESS TU CHIN

ONE AFTERNOON Grandmother Ling crossed the inner courtyard and entered the low house where Yu Lang and her brother lived with their old nurse, Wang Lai. It was the hour for the little girl to have new bindings put on her feet. The Old Old One always directed Wang Lai at such times. She knew just how the bindings could be drawn tight with the least possible pain.

"But it does hurt, Lao Lao," Yu Lang cried out. She was biting her underlip hard in a brave effort not to cry. But Wang Lai was bending her four small toes back under the sole of her foot, and she was pushing her heel and her great toe tightly together while she wrapped the firm bandage around them. Even with Grandmother Ling's great care Yu Lang's poor little feet ached.

"O-yo, I know, Precious Flower," her grandmother said, patting the girl's hand, "but what else can we do? How should you get a good husband if your feet were not tiny like those of a lady? Do not cry, Yu Lang, and I will tell you a story that will make you forget all about your poor feet."

The old woman had her chair moved close to the brick bed upon the edge of which Yu Lang was sitting. And while Wang Lai's old yellow fingers moved about with the binding, she began to speak.

"The first binding of feet by Chinese ladies like us does not lie within my memory, my little Yu Lang, nor even within the memory of my great-great-grandmother. Many tales are told about how small feet came to be the fashion in the Flowery Kingdom. Some say it happened like this. Others say it happened like that. But I will tell you a story my grandmother told me. She declared that it all began with the big feet of the Empress Tu Chin.

"In the earliest days, it seems, Precious Pearl, all the ladies of our land had feet like farm women, feet that were allowed to grow like those of their brothers. Indeed, in those days large feet were thought far more beautiful than small ones.

"In the histories it is said that at that time there lived an Emperor whose name was Ying Shun and who had a wife named Tu Chin whom he loved very dearly. The

Empress was beautiful, and she was noted far and wide over the land for her elegant feet, which were a full twelve inches long. The Emperor Ying Shun preferred his Tu Chin above all the other lovely maids of the palace. He left her side only when it was necessary for him to talk to his ministers about the affairs of the empire.

"Now at night the Emperor Ying Shun slept very soundly. Once the dragons of sleep had carried his soul upward on a voyage to heaven nothing could wake him. The Empress Tu Chin also slept soundly. The moment she laid her head on her pillow she closed her beautiful eyes and fell fast asleep. She knew nothing more until her waiting maids wakened her in the morning.

"But, my precious, the Empress Tu Chin had one very bad habit. She walked in her sleep. Again and again the servants saw the lovely Empress in her night robes of silk, passing silently through the halls of the palace. They knew she was asleep, for she looked neither to the one side nor to the other. Her eyes were wide open, it is true, but they stared straight ahead and they saw nothing. Once a servant on guard held his flickering candle in front of her face. Her eyes did not even blink.

"Everyone knew how greatly the Son of Heaven loved his Empress Tu Chin. And since she always returned safely to the imperial bedchamber, no one breathed a word about her journeys by night. But one day the Emperor came upon two of the palace maid servants whispering to each other, and he thought that he heard one of them mention the name of the Empress.

" 'What do you say, O Twittering Swallows?' he asked.

" 'It is nothing, True Dragon,' the maids replied, frightened.

" 'I heard you speak clearly the name of Her Majesty. I demand to know what you were saying,' the Emperor said sternly. But the poor maids were silent.

" 'Speak, foolish creatures,' he cried, 'or I shall send for the ax and your heads shall come off.'

" 'O Son of Heaven,' one of the maids stammered, trembling, 'it is only that during the night I saw our shining Empress walking in her sleep through the halls of the palace.'

" 'It often happens, Glorious Majesty,' the other maid said. 'She knows not how she goes, for she is indeed fast asleep.'

"The Emperor was troubled. He had heard of such things. But he decided that he would watch for himself before he spoke to Tu Chin. So that night he only pretended to sleep. By great effort he kept himself wide-awake while the lovely Tu Chin slept by his side. Nothing happened, however. A whole hour passed. The Emperor had just decided that the maids must have been lying and that he might as well go to sleep, when he felt the silk coverlids move. He lay very still. Through his half-closed eyes he saw the Empress climbing down from the bed.

"By her movements he, too, could tell that she was still fast asleep. And thinking that she might do herself harm by a misstep, he decided to follow her. So quietly did the Empress walk, and so silent were the steps of the Emperor, that no one in the palace was waked from his slumber. The royal pair had gone a long way when the Emperor decided that he had best end the journey. He threw one arm around the waist of his Empress. At the same time he laid his other hand over her mouth, lest her wakening scream should raise the whole palace. Tu Chin was frightened, and she struggled and struggled until she discovered that it was the Emperor who held her. Then she was no longer afraid, and she allowed him to lead her back to their apartment.

" 'Oh, my heart's treasure,' Ying Shun said to his wife, 'why did you never tell me that you walked in your sleep? I would have had a golden band made to fit round your ankle, and with a golden chain I would have fastened you tight to your bed. I myself would have been the keeper of the key, for I love you so dearly that I would not have you run into danger.'

" 'Ai, Most Great and Glorious One,' poor Tu Chin cried, 'ever since I was a child I have walked in my sleep. But I had hoped that, by the side of your sacred person, I should be safe from the spirits that call me out of my bed in the dark night.'

" 'We shall run no more risks,' the Emperor said as he fastened his girdle about the waist of his Empress and tied it securely to the side of the bed.

"Next morning the Emperor unfastened the girdle and, as soon as the morning rice had been eaten, he spoke to his lady. 'Do you remember, my cherished one, what took place during the night?' he asked.

" 'I remember a dream,' Tu Chin confessed, 'and it was a frightening dream. It seemed that you, my lord, had been away on a journey to a far land, and that you were returning. I seemed to be going forth from the palace across the country to meet you. Deep canals lay on each side of the road. Suddenly out of their water there arose a great dragon. It flew toward me and wound its coils round my waist. I was about to call out to you for help when it put its great paw over my mouth. Then I must have awakened, for I found that the great dragon was yourself and that the paw was your hand.'

" 'Do not fear, my little one,' the Emperor said, comforting her, 'we shall surely find a way to cure you of your unfortunate habit. But it would help greatly if we could only find out what causes you to roam about in the night.'

" 'Alas, I do not know what it could be,' Tu Chin replied, 'unless it should be my feet. All the day through I sit in the palace or on a bench in the garden. My feet are large. It may be that they do not have enough walking during the day, and thus they insist upon walking at night.'

"The Empress spoke proudly of her large feet. They were one of her greatest charms. Indeed, it was chiefly because of their size that the Emperor had chosen Tu Chin as his wife.

"But much as the Emperor admired his wife's feet, he

did not like the idea of their taking her hither and yon during the dark night.

" 'It is quite clear,' he said, 'we must have your feet shortened. If they are but a third as long as they are now, they will need to do only a third as much walking. Then they will not take you out of your bed in the midst of the night.'

"So the Emperor called upon the cleverest doctor in all the Flowery Kingdom. He took eight inches off of each of the Empress's feet. Poor Tu Chin cried because of her small feet, just as you cry, my Yu Lang. But she cried not because of the pain, for her feet healed very quickly. No indeed, she cried because she thought small feet so ugly!

" 'I shall be the laughingstock of the land,' she wept. 'I shall not dare to set foot outside my apartment. I could not bear to see the beautiful large feet of the other maids of the palace. I wish I were dead.'

" 'I shall arrange all that for you, O Daughter of Heaven,' the Emperor said. And he sent forth the order that every maid at the court and every lady in the Empire should make her feet just as small as those of Tu Chin. He commanded all mothers to bind the feet of their daughters, just as we bind yours, Precious Pearl. And from that time to this, small feet have been the fashion in the Flowery Kingdom."

"That is a good story, Lao Lao; I have almost forgotten that my poor feet are aching," Yu Lang said, and she slid down from the bed and tried to take a few steps with her newly bound feet. Tears came to her eyes. But she brushed them away and said Chinese words that sounded like, "O-yo, Mei-yu-fah-dz" and which meant, "Oh well, it cannot be helped!" And she even smiled as she went out into the courtyard to watch Ah Shung and his boy cousins spin tops and play games.

XI

THE GRATEFUL FOX FAIRY

Huang ying, Grandmother Ling's number one maid, was hanging a picture on the gray wall of the old woman's apartment. She had just taken down a painting of a man in red robes sitting sideways upon the back of a smiling tiger. From their places on the brick bed Ah Shung and Yu Lang watched her with interest as she hung in its place a long strip of silk, pasted on paper, upon which was painted a mountain that rose high over the clouds. A winding road led up its side, and men and women with staffs in their hands were toiling along it.

"That is the holy Eastern Mountain, Tai Shan," the Old Old One said to the children. "At the four corners of our world, and in its very center, my little ones, there are high mountains that join the earth with the heavens. But of all the five holy mountains, Tai Shan is the holiest. On its top, rising there above the mist, is a temple to the Jade Emperor, Yu Huan, the greatest of all the gods of the heavens. And not far from its base is the tomb of our great teacher, Confucius, the most perfect and the wisest man who ever lived in our land."

"And who are the men and women climbing the mountain, Lao Lao?" Yu Lang asked, as she slipped down from the bed and toddled across the room to inspect the painting more closely.

"They are good pilgrims who have come many miles to say their prayers in the temples of the Eastern Mountain. They will climb the hundreds of steps which men call the Heavenly Ladder and which lead to the mountaintop, where one can almost look into the Jade Emperor's sky kingdom. Only the rich ride up in those chairs, borne by four sturdy porters.

"Some of those pilgrims will visit one temple," Grandmother Ling continued. "Some will visit another. But no one of them, I think, will forget to kowtow to Niang Niang, the Goddess of Tai Shan, who rules the fox fairies."

"Fox fairies!" Ah Shung and Yu Lang breathed the words with hushed voices. They had heard of fox fairies ever since they were as small as their baby cousin, Lung-Er. They knew that the foxes were the cleverest of all the animals and that they could change themselves into men and women whenever they liked. They knew, too, that fox fairies brought good luck if they were pleased and bad luck if they were angry. There was a tiny temple to the foxes out in their own Garden of Sweet Smells. When good luck did not come, Grandmother Ling often lit sticks of sweet-smelling incense or put small bowls of food in the fox fairies' shrine.

"Did you ever meet a fox fairy, Lao Lao?" Ah Shung asked his grandmother.

"Ai, Bear Boy, I cannot say," the old woman replied. "Who can tell fox fairies from everyday folk? There may be fox fairies inside our own walls at this very hour. That new maid in your uncle's court and the old beggar who is even now eating his rice just inside our red gate may be foxes who have taken the shapes of a young girl and an old man. We could not tell the difference any easier than Yang Le."

"Who was Yang Le, Grandmother?" Ah Shung asked. And Yu Lang hurried back to settle herself, cross-legged, on the brick bed again to listen to the story which she was sure was about to begin.

"Yang Le, Little Curious, was the son of a general, so the tale says," Grandmother Ling began, smiling at the two eager children on the brick bed. "When he was about eighteen years of age his parents both died, and he went to live in the courts of his father's cousin, whose name was Wen Sing.

"Now Wen Sing had a daughter, Mai Mai, who was as fair as the plum blossom for which she was named. She was a good girl. She had been brought up with care and she had been taught all the rules for maidenly behavior. An aunt who was her governess watched over her by day and slept beside her by night. Mai Mai never set foot outside the inner courts except to walk in the garden with her aunts or her girl cousins.

"So Yang Le only saw his pretty cousin, Mai Mai, on family feast days or when he came upon her in the garden in the midst of a group of women and girls. But at their very first meeting he looked upon her with delight. She was so beautiful, he thought, that the flowers in the garden must hang their heads in shame when she passed. He thought she looked at him as though she, in her turn, found him pleasing, and he longed for a chance to speak to her alone.

"But that, of course, was not possible, and so he contented himself with sitting in his lonely room and writing poems about her. He wrote about her smooth brow as white as the rice flour, about her eyebrows as fine as a butterfly's feelers, and about her red lips which were like a pair of ripe cherries. So many verses he wrote that it would take us two days to read them.

"One hot night in summer, when all the Wen family had gone to their beds, Yang Le could not sleep. 'I'll just go into the garden for a breath of fresh air,' he thought to himself. As he walked along the paths in the moonlight he saw a graceful figure coming toward him. He could scarcely believe his eyes when he saw that it had the face of the lovely Mai Mai.

" 'Of course I should not have left my room without telling my aunt,' she said to him shyly. 'But the night is so hot, and I thought there would be a breeze in the garden.' Yang Le and Mai Mai talked for a long time under the trees, and the young man discovered that his pretty cousin loved him quite as much as he cared for her.

" 'But my father will never consent to our marriage,' the maiden told Yang Le sadly. 'He has already promised me to the son of a neighbor.'

"But, in spite of that, Yang Le came secretly each night to the garden, and each night the maiden met him under the trees. None knew of their meeting until the old watchman heard their voices one night. He peeped through the gate into the garden where he saw the two lovers, and he went straight away to tell his master, Wen Sing.

" 'How is this?' Wen Sing cried angrily to the aunt who took care of his daughter. 'You are indeed a fine governess. Do you not know that if you leave the cage open the bird will fly out the door?'

" 'But, Honorable Brother, it could not have been your daughter who was with Yang Le in the garden. Every night she has slept on the inner side of the bed. Again and again I have wakened and looked to see that she was safely sleeping beside me.'

"When they questioned Mai Mai, she would not speak. She only hung her head. Indeed, she did love Yang Le and she would say nothing that might cause him to be beaten. Wen Sing shook his head. He could not understand it at all. 'However it may be, we must send Yang Le away,' he declared to his wife. So he gave the lad money, and he put him outside the gate.

"For many days Yang Le wandered, seeking a shelter. At last he came to an old tower with seven small curving roofs, rising one over the other. It was a pagoda, just like the one that stands on the hill outside our city. No one was living in it, and so the young man decided to make it his home.

"One day a fine sedan chair stopped before the pagoda door. To Yang Le's surprise when its curtain was raised, out stepped the lovely Mai Mai, clad in a red bridal gown. The porters had unpacked all her rich belongings before the young man could recover from his surprise.

" 'I have been brought here by my uncle, Chu, who is the general of this region,' Mai Mai explained to Yang Le. 'My father has consented that I should become your wife. We shall be happy together.'

"Now Yang Le was troubled by such a strange happen-

ing. But he knew that her uncle, Chu, was indeed com-
manding the region, and he rejoiced in his good fortune.
He decided that he would go and thank General Chu for
his kindness in escorting his bride from her home.

" 'But I did not bring my niece with me!' General Chu
cried. 'She is still with her parents. If she had come here,
I am sure my brother would have told me.' He went with
Yang Le to the pagoda to see the bride for himself, and he
was struck dumb with astonishment when he saw that she
was indeed the lovely Mai Mai.

"Not long thereafter, General Chu returned to the city
where the Wen family lived. He made haste to seek his
brother, Wen Sing, and to tell him that he had seen his
daughter, Mai Mai, in Yang Le's pagoda.

" 'That could not be,' Wen Sing declared. 'My daughter has not set foot outside our gate. What can this mean?'
In dismay he called for his wife and the aunt who watched
over Mai Mai, and he told them the news.

" 'It is clear,' said the mother, 'this other Mai Mai is a
fox fairy who takes the form of our daughter. Ai-yah, she
will make everyone believe that our girl gads about in this
scandalous fashion. There is but one thing to do. Call back
Yang Le. Let him marry our daughter!'

"Wen Sing and his brother agreed that this was the only
way to undo the damage. So Yang Le was sent for, and
soon he arrived with his bride. When they entered the
family hall the young man's eyes almost fell out of his
head, for there, standing beside a table, he saw another

Mai Mai. The two maidens were as like as two grains of rice. There was not a hair's difference between them. Even Wen Sing and his wife could not tell which was their daughter.

" 'It is that one who is the daughter of the Wen family,' said the maiden who had entered the hall by the side of Yang Le. 'She is your bride. I am a fox fairy. Many years ago General Yang Han—your grandfather, young man— was out hunting deer on a mountainside near my cave. I was struck by an arrow shot from his bow, and his porters seized me. But the good general, your grandfather, dressed my bleeding wound, and he set me free. I have never forgotten, and now through you, Yang Le, I have paid my debt to him.

" 'I heard that you loved this maiden,' the fox fairy continued as the Wen family stood speechless, 'and I knew you would not be permitted to wed her, even though the old man who lives in the moon long ago joined your ankle to hers with the red cord of marriage. So I took a hand in the matter. I have already reached an age of more than one thousand years and so I can take the shape of a maiden whenever it pleases me. It was I who met you in the garden and who there spoke for Mai Mai. It was I who came in the sedan chair to your pagoda. My plan has succeeded. You are to marry Mai Mai. My work is now done. I shall not see you again.'

"With these words the false Mai Mai disappeared. In her place there was only a little red fox who turned a quick somersault. Sparks rose as its tail struck the stone floor, and it flew out of the room through a crack in the wall.

"And that very day," Grandmother Ling ended her story, "the Wen family gathered in the Hall of the Ancestors to see Yang Le and Mai Mai eat their wedding rice and drink their wedding wine in proper fashion."

XII

LADY WITH THE HORSE'S HEAD

O HONORABLE LADY with the Horse's Head, give leaves to our mulberry trees and health to our silkworms!"

Grandmother Ling spoke these words in a sing-song voice while she swayed back and forth on her knees. In front of her, on the center of a shining black table, was a carved wooden statue of a young woman with a horse's skin thrown over her head and her shoulders. And in a bronze urn before the little statue there burned several sticks of incense that perfumed the air with sweet smoke.

It was spring. The green dragon had awakened from his long winter sleep under the waters and had flown up into the blue sky. The paving stones in the courtyards were marked off from each other by thin lines of green grass. There were spring blossoms in the Garden of Sweet Smells, and birds sang in the branches of the green-tipped willow trees. It was the Third Day of the Third Moon in the Chinese calendar, which falls in the month of April of western lands. This day was the time for worshipping the Silkworm Maiden, and it was before her statue that the Old Old One was saying her little prayer.

Out in the country, beyond the city walls, there were many fields belonging to the Ling family. And on these, among the other crops, grew mulberry trees with whose leaves the Lings fed the tiny gray worms which spun silk for them each year.

"The Daughter of Heaven, our Dragon Empress in Peking, kneels to the Silkworm Maiden and says prayers for the silkworms all over the Empire. So also should we, if we want our leaves to be tender and our worms to spin fine silk," Grandmother Ling explained to Yu Lang and Ah Shung when she rose from her knees and walked out into the spring sunshine.

The air was so soft and warm that the old woman sat down for a few moments on a sunny stone bench beside the door of the family hall. The boy and the girl sat down beside her and began to ask her questions about the silkworms. Would there be as many silkworms hatched inside their red gate as there were last year? Would the women servants keep the eggs warm inside their wadded gowns as at the last hatching season? Which house would be the warmest for the wicker trays covered with tender mulberry leaves upon which the wee baby worms would be put to feed?

Ah Shung and Yu Lang were always interested in the silkworms. They grew so fast, and they changed so quickly from tiny threadlike black creatures to fat gray worms several inches in length. The children liked to hear the worms crunch away at the mulberry leaves. But best of all they liked to see them throw the fine silvery thread out of their mouths and wind it about their own bodies, making little round balls of silk. Their grandmother had told Ah Shung and Yu Lang how the men to whom she sold the silk balls baked them and boiled them and unwound their fine strands.

"Why does the Silkworm Maiden have a horse's skin over her shoulders, Lao Lao?" Yu Lang asked as she sat on the stone bench swinging her little bound feet back and forth, back and forth.

"There's a story about that, Little Precious," said old Grandmother Ling. "In ancient times there lived a young princess whom we now call Tsan Nu, or the Lady of the Silkworms. As all good children should, she loved her father and mother above all else in the world. One day, when she was about fifteen years old, a band of wicked men rode into the palace gate and carried the Emperor away. Poor Tsan Nu was sad at the thought of her father in the hands of the robbers. She would not eat. She would not sleep. She spent most of her time out in the stable with her father's favorite horse because it, too, was waiting for the Emperor to return.

"The Empress grew alarmed at her daughter's condition. She feared that, unless her father returned, the princess would die. So she let it be known that she would make the Princess Tsan Nu the bride of anyone who should bring back the Emperor safe and sound.

"All the young men in the Empire, rich ones and poor ones, set forth to seek for the lost Emperor in the hope that they might win the Princess Tsan Nu. But ai, my children, each one returned with downcast head and shamed face. No one could find him. A whole year went by. Tsan Nu's father was still missing.

"Then one day, when the princess went to the stable to visit her father's favorite horse, she stroked the animal's neck and said, 'You share my sadness, I know. You who have carried my dear father on your back, can you not tell me where he is now? My mother has offered to give me as wife to the one who shall bring my father back safe and sound. But no one can find him, oo-yoo, oo-yoo.' And the poor little princess burst into tears.

"Suddenly to her surprise the horse gave a mighty tug at the strap that fastened him in his stall. He burst it in two. Before the men servants could catch him he galloped away out of the stable and out of their sight. It was no more than two days before the horse came trotting again through the gates of the palace. And riding upon his back was his master, the Emperor, home again safe and sound.

"What rejoicing there was then in the palace! The princess began to eat and to sleep, and she sang all day long because of her father's return. In every court of the palace there was gladness, except in that one where the horses were kept. There the Emperor's favorite steed, who had brought him back safely, never stopped whinnying. It would not eat, and it neighed so loudly that the Empress could hear its cries in her room on the innermost court.

"'I am troubled, O Son of Heaven,' she said to the Emperor. 'While you were gone, our daughter grew so thin with grief that I feared for her life. So I let it be known that I would give her as bride to that one who should bring you back safe and sound. Could that be the reason why your good horse is unhappy? Could it be that he wishes the princess himself?'

"The Emperor laughed. 'Absürd to think that a princess could spend her life with a horse,' he said to the Empress. 'A promise made to men cannot be claimed by a horse.'

"The men servants placed the choicest grain in the manger of the Emperor's horse. But the animal would not touch it. He kept on neighing and whinnying until at last the Emperor lost patience. He called for his bow and he shot a sharp arrow into the side of the horse. He ordered his stablemen to take off the skin of the horse and to lay it to dry on the stones of the courtyard.

"It happened that the Princess Tsan Nu crossed the courtyard where the horse's hide lay. As she stood for a moment beside it, the skin suddenly quivered. It rose from the ground and wrapped itself round her. More swiftly than lightning runs from one cloud to another, it flew up into the heavens and disappeared with the princess.

"Again sadness filled the palace. Day after day the Emperor and the Empress looked up at the sky in the hope that the horse's skin would bring back their daughter. But for ten whole days nothing happened. Then one morning a servant came running to find his royal master.

"'The horse's skin has returned, O Shining One,' he said, breathing hard. 'I saw it with my own eyes at the foot of the mulberry tree in the garden. And the princess is still inside the skin, for I saw her red robe.'

"The Emperor and the Empress and all the men and maids of the court ran to the mulberry tree. They arrived just in time to see the Princess Tsan Nu step out of the horse's skin. But before they had time to speak to her or touch her, she turned into a gray worm and fell to eating the leaves of the mulberry tree.

"In wonder her parents watched her. They came every day to see if she was still there. They begged her to take back the shape of their daughter, but she only went on chewing the tender green leaves. Then one day, when they came, they saw that she was winding herself in shining thread which she threw out of her worm's mouth. In a very short time she had quite disappeared. In their eagerness to

"It happened that the Princess, then five, cried the

"Look at that cloud!" cried the Emperor. "There in the center. Is not that our dear daughter?"

find her again, even in the shape of a worm, they tried in vain to unwind the fine strands of the little house which she had spun for herself. Men say this shining thread that Tsan Nu spun was the very first silk.

"The Emperor and the Empress grieved for their daughter. Each day they sat sadly in the palace garden and wept. One morning, as they were weeping harder than ever, the Emperor happened to look up at the sky overhead.

" 'Look at that cloud!' he cried to his Empress. 'There in the center. Is not that our dear daughter riding my wretched horse? And see, she is followed by a long train of servants!'

"It was indeed Tsan Nu. She flew down to earth and rode the horse into the garden. 'Do not weep for me, dear parents,' she said to her father and mother. 'The Jade Emperor has called me to live in his Heavenly Kingdom. Because of my love for my dear father he has made me a princess in his own palace. He has set me to watch over the worms that spin silken thread like that which I made under the mulberry tree. To you he gives the task of teaching our people how to make silk. You must unwind the tiny strands which my silkworms will spin, and you must twist them together into strong thread. Then there shall be made here in our country cloth so shining and fine that no other can equal it.

" 'Have no fear for me, Honored Parents,' Tsan Nu said in parting. 'In the Heavenly Kingdom I shall live forever and ever, and I shall be happy in my care of the silkworms.' She bowed to her parents. The horse switched his tail and they both disappeared into the clouds.

"That is why, my treasures, the statue of Tsan Nu always shows her as the Silkworm Princess, with a horse's skin thrown over her head and her shoulders. It is because of this story that she has been given her other name: 'Lady with the Horse's Head.' And it is because the Jade Emperor put her in charge of the silkworms that we pray to her in the spring when the leaves on the mulberry trees are green and when the seller of silkworm eggs knocks at our gate."

XIII

THE KING OF THE MONKEYS

ONE sunny spring morning Grandmother Ling stepped through the gate in the white wall that was shaped like a flower vase and that led into the Garden of Sweet Smells beyond the family courts. Ah Shung and Yu Lang and several of the other children followed her. They walked along the main paths, which were paved with little stones arranged in neat patterns. On one of these the pebbles were fitted together to form daisies, on another they made a long twisting dragon. The smaller paths were of earth packed hard and smooth.

The Lings loved their garden. At each season of the year there were different flowers and shrubs in the gay china pots that were set along its winding paths. Little dwarf pine trees with twisted brown trunks were green summer and winter, and other evergreen bushes, trimmed to curious shapes, lined the garden walks. Here was a bush shaped like a fish, with china eyes added to make it more real. Nearby was a huge evergreen bird, and along down the path there was a bush cut like a basket. Ah Shung liked best the two little trees on either side of the pathway which were trimmed to look like two old Chinese gentlemen. Bits of wood formed their heads, their hands, and their feet. The boy often made them low bows as he walked past.

Ah Shung and Yu Lang were carrying red bird cages shaped like pagodas. Inside were tiny yellow singing birds, favorite pets of their father. Each fair day the birds were taken for a walk through the Garden of Sweet Smells and their cages hung up on the limb of a tree, where they sang even louder than the wind bells under the ends of the curving tiled roofs of the family dwellings.

"Spring has wakened the goldfish. How they dart about

under the lily pads!" Yu Lang cried as the little procession stopped on the white bridge that rose in a half circle over the lotus pool. Its water reflected their faces like a mirror as they looked down at the fat red dragon-eyed fish with their long phoenix-tails.

"Oh, see the peach trees," the Old Old One exclaimed. "They have blossomed since yesterday." On the arm of her faithful maid, Huang Ying, she hurried past the tiny mountain, built up of rocks and mossy earth, to the little summer house at the very end of this garden path. Beside the open pavilion were two flowering peach trees whose branches almost touched its roofs of curving green tile. Each little brown bud seemed to have burst in the night, for the trees were covered with clouds of pink blossoms.

"We shall sit here in our summer house and view the peach blossoms," the Old Old One said to the children. "How like the sunset they are! How fortunate for us that our peach trees are not as that one in the kingdom of the Empress of the West!"

"Why, Lao Lao?" asked Ah Shung. "Why are our peach trees better than hers?"

"Because, Little Bear, our trees blossom each spring, while her tree turns pink only once in three thousand years. Sit quietly here and I will tell you about it.

"Far, far to the west are the mountains of Kun Lun. So high do they rise into the air that snow covers their peaks all the year through. But at their feet there is warmth and beauty and splendor. Bushes whose branches are laden with pearls grow beside trees whose leaves are of precious green jade stone. Near a lake, whose crystal waters lap shores covered with gems, stands the Western Empress's great peach tree.

"Now this tree of hers is three hundred miles around and the peaches it bears—how can I show you how enormous they are? If Ah Shung will make a circle with his two arms, just touching his finger tips, that circle will be no larger than this fairy fruit. More wonderful still, whoever eats of this fruit will never die. He will live forever. Because of this fact we think a peach of some kind is the very best birthday gift. When we send our friends peaches they know we are wishing that they will live a long time."

"Who dwells in the Kun Lun Mountains, Lao Lao?" Yu Lang asked her grandmother.

"All the people who have eaten the peaches-of-long-life live there with the Western Empress, whom men call Si Wang Mu. Fair princesses wait upon her, and all in her court wear robes of the most splendid silk of the brightest of colors. The long-life ones walk in beautiful gardens, among white marble palaces. In one place there is a nine-storied pagoda made of red jasper stone. When we return to the courtyards I will unroll before you a scroll which shows Si Wang Mu with the white crane upon which she rides through the sky. She holds a huge long-life peach in her hand, for she is the guardian of this wonderful peach tree, and she alone may pluck its fruit.

"Every three thousand years Si Wang Mu's peach tree

blossoms. And it is three thousand years more before its fruit is ripe. As soon as the peaches are ready the Royal Mother of the West celebrates her birthday with a great banquet. She spreads her table beside a fountain which drips shining jewels, on the shores of the Gem Lake. What food she brings forth! Rich meat, rare fruits, the peaches-of-long-life! Bears' tongues, dragon livers, and phoenix eggs! Nothing could be finer than Si Wang Mu's birthday feast. Only once was it spoiled, and that was because of the wicked King of the Monkeys."

"Tell us about that, Lao Lao," the children cried as their grandmother paused in her tale.

"Well, that Monkey King was a mischievous creature. No doubt the Jade Emperor meant well when he brought him into the world, but he was sorry later on, that I can tell you. The old books say this monkey was born on the rocky side of a mountain, far to the east. At first he was only a stone shaped like a monkey. Then the Emperor of Heaven put life into his body, and he breathed and moved.

" 'This monkey shall give pleasure to the mountains,' the Jade Emperor said. 'He shall leap from one peak to another. He shall ride on the winds. He shall walk through the sea. He shall live in the caves high in the hills, and he shall eat the fruit of the trees that grow on their sides. Of all the beasts on the mountains he shall be cleverest.'

"With such gifts from heaven, my children, it is not at all strange that this fairy creature soon became King of the Monkeys. He learned to dress himself like a man, although he could not get rid of his furry face. With one jump he could travel from one end of the earth to the other, and he could fly even as high as the Jade Emperor's palace in the Heavenly Kingdom. People called him Sun Wu Kung, the One-Who-Finds-Out-All-Secrets.

"During one of Sun's journeys he came to the palace of the mighty Lung Wang, the King of the Dragons, who lives under the sea.

" 'What is the most wonderful thing in all your realm, O Dragon King?' Sun asked politely.

" 'It is this,' Lung Wang replied, showing Sun a slender iron rod. 'The great Emperor Yu himself put this rod here to keep the sea waters level. It is a magic rod. It can become long enough to reach from earth into heaven, or it can shrink to the size of a needle, half an inch long, which you could easily hide behind your ear. By means of it wishes come true and miracles happen.'

"Without warning, the wicked Monkey King pulled the iron rod out of its place, and with one leap he escaped from the Sea Dragon's realm. As he passed through the water kingdoms he seized silks and gems with which to deck himself out, and when he appeared upon earth again he looked so very fine that seven kings were eager to have him for their friend. They made him a feast at which Sun drank and ate so much that he fell fast asleep.

"Now the Dragon King was angry at the loss of the magic rod that held the sea waters level. He sent after the thief and had him seized during his slumber. But as soon as he woke, Sun used the magic rod and set himself free.

"So much mischief was done by the wicked King of the Monkeys that his fame spread over the earth from the east to the west and from the north to the south. He feared no one, not the Jade Emperor himself. It is said that in one fit of temper he even upset the Emperor's throne and broke down the South Gate of his Heavenly Kingdom. He boldly declared that in due time he, Sun, would become the Ruler of Heaven.

"In order to quiet him, the Jade Emperor gave this wicked King of the Monkeys a splendid post in his kingdom, and he built him a palace almost as fine as his own. Now at just about this time it so happened that the fruit-of-long-life on the peach tree in the Kun Lun Mountains was ready for eating, and Si Wang Mu was preparing for her great birthday banquet. To her Feast of the Peaches the Western Empress invited all the gods and the goddesses who lived in the Heavenly Kingdom. But she did not invite Sun, the wicked King of the Monkeys.

"When he heard of the feast Sun grew very angry. In a fury he set forth for the mountains of Kun Lun, his magic rod in his hand. When all was in readiness for the birthday feast he laid a spell upon the whole kingdom. Everyone, men servants and maid servants, princes and princesses, and even the Royal Mother herself, fell into a deep sleep.

"There was only one guest at that birthday table, and that guest was Sun. He ate the fairy peaches and all the best foods. He drank the best wines. So much did he eat and drink that he could not think clearly, and on his way back to heaven he took the wrong turning. Somehow or other he came to the palace of the great teacher, Lao Chun, who just then was away from home on a long journey. Now Sun knew that Lao Chun had in his keeping some of the heavenly pills which, like the peaches of Kun Lun, will make men live forever.

"In the time that it takes to swallow a mouthful of tea the wicked King of the Monkeys found those pills-of-long-life hidden in gourds. He gulped down one just as he had eaten the peach-of-long-life at the birthday feast of Si Wang Mu. He was happy indeed because he was now doubly sure of living forever.

"How angry the gods were when they heard of these deeds of the wicked King of the Monkeys! The Jade Emperor summoned his warriors, and Sun called to his aid all the troops of his monkey army. The gods spread a net across the broad heavens. What a battle they fought! But still they could not conquer Sun. Then Lao Chun, the wise teacher, whose pill had been stolen, and every god in the Heavenly Kingdom joined in the fight. At last the monkey army was driven into the net. But Sun was not taken. By the aid of his iron rod he had changed himself into a cloud and floated safely away.

"Well, my small ones, it is a long tale. Each time Sun was captured he would make his magic rod small and hide it behind his ear. With it in his possession he could always change his shape and escape. Then too, nothing could kill

him, neither sword, fire, nor lightning because, you remember, he had eaten the peach and he had swallowed the pill
which gave him the power of living forever.

"At last, in despair, the Jade Emperor called upon the
greatest god of them all, Buddha, to whose red-roofed
temple in the city we go so often to pray.

"'How dare you think of yourself as the Ruler of
Heaven?' Buddha said to the Monkey King.

"'I have power enough,' was the bold monkey's reply.

"'There are those more powerful than you,' Buddha
said calmly. 'What have you beside power?'

"'I cannot die. I can change myself into seventy-two
different shapes. I can ride on the winds and I can walk
through the sea. In one jump I can travel from one end of
the earth to the other.'

"'And yet,' Buddha said, 'you cannot go further than
the palm of my hand. Let us make a bargain. If you can go
out of my reach I will indeed make you the Ruler of
Heaven.'

"The Monkey King made a mighty leap. Before you
could blink your eyes, my children, he had flown to the
other end of the earth. There on the red pillar that holds
up the heavens he wrote his name so as to show he had
really been there. Then he returned to face Buddha.

"'Now make me the Ruler of Heaven,' the Monkey
King cried.

"'No, Foolish One,' Buddha said, 'You have not yet
left the palm of my hand.'

" 'How can that be?' the Monkey King cried. 'I set down my name on the red pillar of heaven at the other end of the earth.'

" 'Still, the words that you wrote are here on my hand,' Buddha said as he held up his forefinger. Sun grew weak and trembled, for he saw that the name he had written on the red pillar of heaven was, indeed, there before him on the finger of Buddha. And he knew that no one could become greater than the god Buddha, who held the whole earth in the palm of his hand.

"It was Buddha who drove the Monkey King out of the Heavenly Kingdom and put him in prison under the five rocky mountains. For while the monkey stood on his palm Buddha suddenly turned his hand upside down with his finger tips firmly set on the earth. The monkey was caught. It was Buddha's own fingers that made the five mountains, so people say. Whether the Monkey King ever got out again I do not know. But I never heard of his spoiling the Feast of the Peaches again."

XIV

TWO DUTIFUL SONS

Aʜ sʜᴜɴɢ! Ah Shung! Your honorable father has work for you in his library. Ah Shung! Ah Shung! Where are you? Come quickly!"

Old Wang Lai, the number one nurse of the Ling family, was calling and calling. She hurried from one courtyard to the other, looking everywhere for the boy. The other maid servants ran out to help her, and at last the Old Mistress herself came to the door of her room to see what the noise meant.

"O Honorable Old Lady, I have looked in the stables, in the entrance court, and in all the family houses. I have searched the Court of Politeness. I have asked Scholar Shih in the House of Learning. I have even gone down the paths in the Garden of Sweet Smells. Nowhere can we find Ah Shung whose father calls for him."

"And the Court of the Ancestors, have you searched there?" the Old Mistress inquired. Her black eyes, usually so calm, were troubled. She feared lest some accident might have befallen her grandson.

The procession of servants followed the Old Mistress through the gateway that led into the Court of the Ancestors. The old woman's sharp eyes darted quickly from this side to that. Suddenly she gave a soft cry. She had spied a red top-cord hanging over the side of a huge blue-and-white porcelain jar that stood in one corner. She hurried across the paving stones and peered into the jar. A small boy with a spinning top in his hand was curled up like a ball inside it. He looked up at her with blinking black eyes like those of a scared rabbit.

"O Worthless Puppy," Grandmother Ling scolded as Wang Lai pulled Ah Shung out of the jar, "it was wicked to cause your old nurse so much trouble. But it was far more wicked to act so toward your father."

The Old Old One's eyes were twinkling but her mouth was stern. Ah Shung had looked comical huddled there in the jar, but to disobey his father was the greatest of sins, and the boy would have to be punished.

"Go to your father at once, naughty boy," said Grandmother Ling, "and when he has done with you, come back here to me. We shall go into the Hall of the Ancestors and you shall kneel down before them and pray for their forgiveness."

The stone floor of the Hall of the Ancestors was hard. Lao Lao made the naughty boy kneel upon it in front of the red tablets and below the scroll paintings of the forefathers. She kept him there until his bones ached. As he kowtowed again and again before his grandfather and his great-grandfather he decided that another time it would be best to go when he was called, especially if it was his father who wanted him.

When his prayers were over and his punishment ended, Grandmother Ling sent him to fetch the other children. She gathered them about her on the veranda just outside her door.

"It is time I spoke to you once again about your duty to your honorable parents," the old woman said. She settled herself in the chair which her maid, Huang Ying, brought her, and arranged her blue silk gown smoothly over her knees. "Duty to parents comes first of all. You may become wise. You may become famous. But if you do not obey and respect your father and mother, the gods will not bring you good luck.

"Our wise teacher, Confucius, used to sing the praises of dutiful sons. He tells us of one who laid down on the ice in order to thaw a hole in the frozen river with the warmth of his own body so that he could get fish for his old mother to eat. He writes of another who went to bed early each night so that the mosquitoes should satisfy their hunger and thirst upon him before his parents came to their rest.

"It pleases the gods, my children, when parents are cared for. Once long ago there lived a poor fisher youth whose old father died. The young man had no money, so he sold all his belongings in order to give his father's spirit a proper start on its journey to the World of Shadows.

"With the money he received from the sale of his belongings the young man bought paper gowns, paper shoes, a paper hat, and even a small paper house. He burned these so that they should go along with the spirit to the Shadowy World. He knew that there, as here on earth, one must have shelter, clothing, and food, and he wished to be sure that his father's spirit should have all of these comforts. He burned heaps of round bits of paper shaped just like coins so that the spirit should have money to buy other things it might need. And he laid his father's coffin in a neat grave mound which he planted with grass and which he tended with care.

"Every morning the young fisherman, who now lived alone, went out in his boat to catch fish from the sea. One day, not long after the funeral, when he drew in his net he found in it a huge shell shaped like a horn. With its creamy outside and its lining of rose, he thought the shell so pretty that he carried it home with him to his hut.

"The next evening when he returned from his fishing he

saw to his surprise that his house had been dusted and the floor had been swept. Bowls of steaming white rice and spicy salt turnips were set out on the table.

" 'Who can have done this for me?' he asked himself. 'No doubt it was some traveler who stopped here to rest and who has repaid me in this way.' But the next evening, also, his hut was swept clean and his dinner was cooked. As the same thing happened day after day, the fisher youth grew more and more curious.

"One morning he did not go to his boat. Instead, he hid outside his hut and peeked in at the window. All was quiet inside. There was no one about. Suddenly he saw a figure rise from the pink-and-white shell. It was a maiden so fair that the room seemed as light as though one hundred candles were burning.

"For a long time the young fisherman watched the maiden busy herself with setting the place in order. Then at last he stepped inside the door.

" 'O Shining Shell Maiden,' he said, 'how come you here in my poor humble hut?'

" 'I come from the Heavenly Kingdom, Excellent Young Sir,' the Shell Maiden replied. 'The Emperor of the Gods was pleased with your unselfishness. As a reward for your respect for your father he has sent me to care for your house and to cook your food for you.'

"Well, of course it was not long before the young fisherman married the lovely Shell Maiden. And he had many sons who cared for him in his old age just as kindly as he had cared for his own father. What better reward could the Heavenly Emperor have given him?

"Ai, my little ones, everyone praises a child who is kind to his parent. Even a thief's heart can be melted by the sight of a dutiful son." Grandmother Ling had just thought of a second story which she wanted Ah Shung and the other children to hear.

"Once a young man, whose name was Ho Lin, lived with his mother. His father had died, and the good young man never stopped grieving for him. Each spring and each autumn he swept his father's grave clean and never forgot to set out food for his spirit when feast days came around. Toward his mother, Ho Lin was as kind and good a son as woman could wish.

"Well, one night a robber came to the little house where Ho Lin lived with his mother. He bound the young man tight to a chair. Then he spread on the floor a square piece of cloth upon which he began to lay out the things he meant to take away with him.

"The thief took Ho Lin's best silk gown out of the treasure chest. But the young man said nothing. The thief took his new shoes with the heavy black satin sides and the clean white soles. But the young man still kept his lips tightly closed. One after another the robber laid on the square cloth all of Ho Lin's most prized possessions. But still the youth remained silent. Only when the thief picked up a copper pan did he speak.

" 'Be good enough, I pray you, to leave me that copper

pan,' Ho Lin said to the robber. 'Take all the rest but leave me that, so that I may have something in which to cook my old mother's breakfast tomorrow morning.'

"The thief was astounded. He dropped the pan on the table. 'Bad luck will surely come to me if I rob so dutiful a son,' he thought to himself.

" 'Not only will I leave you the copper pan, O Young Sir of Such Remarkable Goodness, but I will leave all your belongings,' he said to Ho Lin. And he went on his way.

"Here again, my dear children, a good son was rewarded because of his respect and care for his old parents."

XV

THE POET AND THE PEONY PRINCESS

ONE AFTERNOON in spring guests came and went through the bright red gate in the wall that surrounded the Ling courtyards. The Old Old One had invited friends to walk through the Garden of Sweet Smells and enjoy the peonies which were then in full bloom. Their shaggy blossoms made the garden gay with their red, pink, and white petals, and they sent a sweet perfume into the air.

The day was sunny and warm. So the Old Mistress had

ordered the maid servants to bring tea and cakes to the round stone table in the center of the garden. There the blossoms could be seen better than in the summer house at the end of the walk.

Yu Lang sat on a curving stone bench with the grown-up guests. Her bound feet hurt her too much to run about with Ah Shung and the boy visitor with whom he was flying kites. The little girl watched the huge paper butterfly and the giant paper fish that floated high above the garden across the blue sky. The boys were pretending these were fighting kites. Once Ah Shung succeeded in hooking his fish behind his visitor's butterfly and in drawing both kites to the ground. But he was not so rude as to suggest that his guest should give him his kite, which would have been his right if they had really been fighting kites, as young men of China so like to do.

"Of all the flower queens, the peony seems to me the most lovely," one guest remarked as she sipped her hot jasmine tea from a handleless cup as thin as an eggshell. In old China each moon or month had a flower as its queen, and one day in early spring was set apart as the Birthday of All the Flowers. At that season, also, parties were given and there were celebrations in the gardens.

"You speak truly, dear friend," said Grandmother Ling. "No flower guests are quite so welcome in my garden as the peony blossoms. With their sunrise colors they drive away the last dark mists which the Black Tortoise of Winter has left behind him. Our peony friends are late in coming this year. I have been impatient. I have felt like the ancient Emperor who tried to hasten the blooming of his flowers by building a glasshouse about them and by sending his musicians to play sweet tunes to them as they opened."

Each spring at her peony party it was Grandmother Ling's custom to show respect to her flower guests with poems and stories.

"Will you not honor us with a flower poem?" she asked the oldest one of her visitors.

"I am unworthy of having first place, Great and Ancient Hostess," the visitor replied, "but I remember some verses about the peony blossoms that were written by a poet of long, long ago."

The visitor repeated charming lines that told of a young man who fell deeply in love with a princess in the Emperor's palace. When the Emperor discovered that the two had been meeting he shut up the princess and forbade her to set foot outside the inner courts. But the princess had heard that the stream which ran across the imperial garden flowed, also, through the garden of her young lover. So she wrote messages to him upon white peony petals which she cast on the water. No one in the palace noticed the floating white petals. But by lucky chance the young man saw the marks of her brush upon one as it floated under his bridge. He captured the petal and read the message it bore. He took heart at this sign that she was waiting for him. He studied well and worked hard to pass the examinations, and he rose to such a high place that in the end the Emperor gave his consent to his marriage with the princess.

Everyone about the stone table was delighted with this poem about the white peony petals. When it was ended the old visitor bowed to Grandmother Ling, saying, "Now that my unworthy voice has been heard, will you not lighten our dark minds with your own learning, Ancient Lady of Great Goodness?"

"I fear that my words will seem like dull garden pebbles beside the shining jade clearness of those you have just spoken," the Old Old One replied. "But, if you wish, I will tell you the story of the poet and the peony princess."

Ah Shung and his playmate had pulled down their kites and had joined the group of children who were sitting with the grownups on the stone benches. Everyone listened in silence as Grandmother Ling began her tale.

"Once in ancient days, near the temple on the Old Mountain, the peonies grew twice as high as a man. Their blossoms were as large as those pots along our paths, and their masses of bright colors made each garden look like a giant piece of embroidery.

"A young poet named Fang built his house on that hillside because he thought the sight of the flowers would help him to make his verses more beautiful. One day, as he looked out of his window, he saw in his garden a fair maiden dressed in a trailing rose-colored robe.

" 'She could not have come from the temple. Only priests may live there,' he thought to himself as he went down

The maiden gave a cry and fled down the path, her rosy robe floating behind her like the tail of a phoenix

the path toward her. But before he could question her, she had disappeared among the peonies.

"On several occasions the young man almost caught up with the maiden in the rose gown who walked in his garden. But each time she vanished before he came near her. Fang could not put the maiden's image out of his mind. When he sat down at his table to write verses, the words would not come. His paper was blank. At last he decided to hide in the garden, in the hope that he might watch her without himself being seen.

"In this way he was able to look full on her face, and he found her as beautiful as the new moon. He stepped from his hiding place and was about to speak to her. But the maiden gave a cry and fled down the path, her rosy robe floating behind her like the tail of a phoenix. Fang ran after her to the end of his garden. Suddenly he was face to face with his own wall, and there was no maiden in sight.

Sadly he returned to the house. He dipped his writing brush in the ink upon his ink stone, and on a piece of white paper he set down this verse:

> "*With trembling heart, fair maid, I call,*
> *Come back within my garden wall.*
> *Some awesome fate for you I fear,*
> *Take care! Take care! For danger's near.*

"He fastened his poem to a tree near the wall where the maid had disappeared. And that very evening, as he sat in his library looking out at the garden, the young girl herself entered his door.

" 'Excellent Sir,' she said, 'you frightened me there in the garden. But that was before I found out that you were a learned scholar who could write beautiful verses.'

" 'And you, Shining Maiden,' said Fang, 'who are you and why are you here on this lonely Old Mountain?'

" 'My name is Siang Yu and my home is far away. But a powerful god forces me to remain here on this hillside.'

" 'Tell me where he lives, and you shall soon be set free,' Fang said, flushing with anger.

" 'No, Excellent Young Man,' the maiden replied, 'I shall be quite happy here, now that I have met such a learned poet as you. If you will not make fun of me, I should like to say for you a verse that has just come into my mind:

> *"Beneath thy roof the hours fly.*
> *Too soon the sun lights up the sky.*
> *O Gracious Moon God, grant that we*
> *Never more may parted be.*

"The maiden hung her head with shame at her bold words, but Fang was filled with joy.

" 'Fair Without and Wise Within, who could fail to love you?' he cried. And as you may easily guess, it was not long until the poet and the maiden were married.

"Now the fair Siang Yu explained that she could not spend all her time under Fang's roof because of the god who kept her on the Old Mountain. However, she came as often as she could, and the two young people were happy.

"Then one day, as she took leave of her poet, Siang Yu's eyes filled with tears. 'Do you remember the verse you pinned to the tree near the wall?' she asked Fang. 'Do you recall that you wrote:

> "*Some awesome fate for you I fear,*
> *Take care! Take care! For danger's near?*"

Well, that time has come. Our life together is ended. I shall not be here tomorrow.'

" 'What is it, my dear one?' Fang asked in dismay. 'Tell me what the danger is and I surely can save you.'

"But his wife would say nothing except, 'It lies in the garden. It lies in the garden!'

"That night Fang had a dream. His soul walked in a garden between tall peony flowers. Suddenly he came upon a workman who was cutting out a new path. The man was digging up a peony plant which had a rose-colored blossom. As he threw the flower to one side it seemed to Fang that its shape changed into that of a maiden and that that maiden had the face of his beloved Siang Yu. He gave such a cry that he woke himself from his slumber.

"The sun had already risen. Fang leaped from his bed, for from his dream he had learned that his dear wife was a flower fairy, a Peony Princess.

" 'Oh, that I may be in time to save her,' he cried as he rushed out of the house and along the paths in the garden.

Down this one, up that one, he went. But all was quiet and still. Then he saw in the distance a figure clad in the blue cotton suit of a gardener. He ran like the wind, and he arrived just as the workman was setting his hoe to the roots of a tall peony plant whose blossom was of the same rose color as the gown Siang Yu always wore.

" 'Stop! Stop!' Fang cried, and he told the gardener his story. The stupid fellow did not believe him at first, but as they stood talking, a bud on the peony began to swell. Before their eyes it grew larger and larger. It opened wider and wider. It was almost as big around as the basket which the gardener carried. And in the nest of its rosy petals there sat a maiden, no more than twelve inches tall, who had the face and figure of the poet's wife. Fang lifted the tiny creature gently from her rosy throne and set her upon her feet on the path. At once she grew to the height of a woman, and he found that she was indeed his beloved Siang Yu.

"Thereafter, the poet and his Peony Princess lived safely together there on the Old Mountain, for Fang built a white wall to shut in the flower upon which his wife's life depended. Even after she died and her plant no longer bloomed, he cared for it tenderly.

"At last, when the time of his own death drew near, he called his son to him.

" 'I shall not die, my son,' Fang said. 'You must not weep. As I slept last night, my soul made a journey to the God of the Flowers, and he has consented that I may be

born again as a peony. Look well at the ground beside
your dear mother's plant inside the white wall. When you
see in the ground there beside it a red shoot with five slender leaves sprouting from it, you may know it is I.'

"It happened as the poet foretold. The red shoot with
the five slender leaves rose from the ground. It grew strong
and tall beside Siang Yu's plant inside the white wall.
So, as she had prayed in the verse which she made on her
first visit, the Peony Princess and her poet were not
parted, even in death."

XVI

THE FIRST EMPEROR'S MAGIC WHIP

THE SKY DRAGONS are having a good battle today. The rain pours like a river out of the clouds," Wang Lai said to the children as they walked along the covered veranda that led round the courtyard to their grandmother's apartment. The old nurse firmly believed that dragons were lashing their tails against the black clouds that covered the sky. She was sure it was their fighting that sent down from the heavens the streams of water that were running over the paving stones of the court-yards and dripping from the turned-up corners of the gray tile roofs.

During this afternoon's hour with their grandmother Ah Shung and Yu Lang looked out at the rain through an open window whose paper-lined panes had been pushed aside to let in the warm air. For a time they talked of this and of that, of Ah Shung's lessons with the writing brush, of Yu Lang's embroidery, of the good things they had eaten with their rice at midday, and of the cakes they would soon be having at tea.

Then Ah Shung walked across the room to look at a shining black chest that stood against the gray wall. Upon its glossy face a country scene was painted, and bits of pearly shell had been set deep in the black lacquer to make the pattern more beautiful.

The scene on the chest showed a broad stretch of land, with tiny women and men, wee houses and trees, and even mountains and rivers. But the thing that interested Ah Shung the most was a wall that wound across the land, up mountains and down valleys, like a twisting dragon.

"What a long wall, Lao Lao," he said, as he ran his finger delicately along its winding course.

"Ai, Little Bear, and the Long Wall is what we call it," the Old Old One replied. "That is a part of the great wall that was built by a famous Emperor who belonged to the family named Chin. It is a story you should know. I will tell it to you.

"In the ancient days, when this Chin Emperor lived, our land was surrounded by unfriendly people. From the north and the west strange robber bands often rode down upon us. So the Son of Heaven decided that he would build a great wall to shut out these foes. He was a true dragon, that Chin Emperor. Men say he was cruel. They say he was a tiger. So indeed was he. He let nothing stand in the way of what he wanted to do. He gave orders to build a wall around our vast land just as we would tell men to lay up a wall round a courtyard.

"'My name shall be called the Only First,' the Tiger Emperor declared. 'Never has there been an Emperor like me.' And he burned all the books that told of the deeds of kings who had lived before him, in order that his own glory should shine the brighter.

"The Long Wall was the greatest thing the Only First built. Just as you see it there on the chest, it runs over our land, up hill and down dale, for many hundreds of miles. As high as the temple roof it rises above the fields, and they say two carts can be driven side by side along its paved top. I have been told that it is really two walls of stone and brick, with earth packed hard between them. Can you see the towers, Ah Shung, where the warriors stand with their bows and their arrows and their cannon, that keep the strangers away? So long as the Walls stands there to protect us, we shall be safe."

"Does the Long Wall truly go about all sides of our land, Lao Lao?" Ah Shung asked his grandmother.

"No, Small Bear, that Chin Emperor did not finish his wall. He intended that it should be shaped like a huge horseshoe, with both ends in the ocean and with our country hugged inside its encircling arms. He began at one end in the Eastern Sea, and he succeeded in building his wall far into the desert at the north. There it ends. There is a story about that too. Men say Chin did not finish the Wall because he lost his magic whip.

"You see, my children," Grandmother Ling explained, "never in all the world has there been such a feat as building the Long Wall. The Only First kept hundreds of thousands of men at work day and night, year after year. He had them whipped when they stopped. But even so, he could never have built the Wall if the gods and the spirits had not come forth to help.

"How could the poor workmen have carried those great stone blocks in baskets on their own backs? How could they have lifted them high up to the top of the Mighty Wall? No, the spirits of the mountains themselves helped to roll the stones into their places, and a magic white horse dashed ahead of the wall builders to lay out the way. You can see there on the chest how he must have climbed rugged cliffs and leaped across deep valleys, as only a fairy steed could. And always the builders followed his lead, laying up their wall zigzag, like a serpent in stone.

"Only once did the wall builders lose their fairy guide,

so the tale goes. The white horse galloped so swiftly they could not keep up with him. At first, when they found he had disappeared from their sight, they did not worry, for they said to each other, 'We can follow his hoof marks.' And they stopped long enough to make tea with which to quench their thirst.

"But even as they drank, there blew down from the Northern Desert a terrible windstorm that covered the land with a thick carpet of dust. The wall builders could not find a single hoof mark of the Emperor's horse, but they went on building the Wall in the direction in which they thought he had gone. Day after day passed, and still they did not catch up with their fairy guide. At last they sent a lookout to the top of a high mountain, and far in the distance he spied the white horse, galloping in quite another direction. So the poor wall builders went back to the place where they had lost him, and they began their work over. This tale must be true, for my honorable father himself once saw this very part of the Wall, shooting off from the main line like the branch of a tree.

"But the most important heavenly gift which the Chin Emperor had to help him was his magic whip. It seems the Jade Emperor looked down from his palace high in the sky, and pitied the toiling wall builders whom Chin treated so cruelly. He secretly gave each workman a magic cord to bind about his wrist and the Only First could not understand why the work went so much faster. The stones flew into place and the men no longer complained.

"When at last the Emperor discovered these magic cords he seized every one of them and he braided them into a long lash for his whip. With this magic whip he forced the mountains to help him. He made the rivers stand still while the Wall crossed their beds. He lashed the rocks until drops of red blood oozed out of their sides. In places these red rocks can be seen to this day.

"All went well with the Wall. On and on it was pushed, over the mountains and far to the north into the great desert.

"Now among the army of wall builders there was a certain prince whom the Emperor hated because he was kind to the workmen. One day this prince disappeared. He was never seen again. At the same time, at his home, his princess wife had a dream that all was not well with her husband. The dream troubled her so that she set out for the Wall, to find out for herself if her husband was safe.

"In a cart which had large wheels fit for travel over rough country she rode and she rode until she came to the place where the wall builders were working. But alas, her husband was not among them, and no one would tell her what had become of him. She decided to seek out the Emperor himself, and so she went to his palace.

" 'O Son of Heaven, O Lord of Ten Thousand Years,' she implored, 'tell me where my dear husband is.'

" 'Ai, there was an accident,' the Emperor replied. 'Your husband was killed when the Wall fell in upon him. But do not fear for yourself, Fair Princess. I find you charming. You shall dwell here in my palace as my most cherished wife.'

"The princess cried out in horror. Something told her that the Tiger Emperor had himself killed her husband and that he would have no more pity upon her in her sorrow than he had on the poor people who toiled on his Wall, day in and day out.

" 'Sooner will I go to the Dragon King,' the princess declared when the Emperor tried to lead her into his inner court. She broke away and threw herself into the lake beside which his splendid palace was built.

"Under the lake the princess soon found herself standing before Lung Wang, the great Dragon King. 'Do you bring news, Princess?' Lung Wang asked. 'Tell me, how goes the Wall that the Emperor is building?'

" 'It goes on and on,' the princess replied. 'With his magic whip the cruel Tiger Emperor drives all before him. And the wall builders die like so many flies. Even my husband has been sent to the World of Shadows because of the Wall. Have pity, good Dragon King. Send one of your spirits to help my poor people.'

" 'Without his magic whip the Emperor could do nothing,' the Dragon King said. 'Now, my wife is beautiful and my wife is clever. I shall send her to the earth to steal the whip from that tiger-man. Then the Wall will be stopped and your people set free.'

"The very next day there appeared in the Emperor's palace a new princess as fair as the pear trees in spring.

She quickly became the Only First's favorite, and he spent all his time away from the Wall in her apartment. With sweet words she flattered him, and with soft music from her fifty-stringed lute she lulled him to sleep.

"The Only First never let his magic whip out of his hand, and he bound it to his wrist whenever he slept. But all things are possible to dragons, Ah Shung, and it did not take the Dragon Queen long to unfasten the knots and to steal the magic whip, as the Dragon King had commanded.

"When the cruel Emperor woke, he found to his horror that his whip had disappeared, and with it the fair princess. All his fury and threats could not bring the magic whip back. The mountains no longer moved at his command. The rivers no longer held their waters back for him. The stones no longer rolled down to the Wall. And so the work stopped and the Wall never was finished."

"Is that story true, Lao Lao?" Yu Lang asked the Old Old One.

"Who knows that, Little Precious?" Grandmother Ling replied, shaking her head. "But to this day the Long Wall stops there in the desert. Other Emperors worked upon it. But none completed the mighty horseshoe of stone and earth which the Only First planned to build."

XVII
THE WONDERFUL PEAR TREE

THE GARDEN OF SWEET SMELLS behind the Ling court-yards was gay with color on this summer afternoon. Flowers of many hues bloomed in the fat porcelain pots set here and there along its neat paths, and pink lotus lilies floated upon the Pool of the Goldfish. But quite as bright as the petals of the garden flowers were the children

in their summer suits of thin cotton and silk. Small
Dragon, the youngest of all the Ling grandchildren,
looked like a giant poppy in his jacket and trousers of
bright red, and the little girls in their pinks, blues, and
greens made Grandmother Ling think of the butterflies
that flitted about in the warm summer sun.

The Old Old One, clad in a pale lavender gown of thin-
nest silk, sat fanning herself upon a stone bench by the
side of the pool. Her slanting black eyes beamed with
pleasure as she watched her grandchildren playing round
its edges.

Ah Shung had just come into the garden. On his way
from the Court of Learning he had stopped in at the little
low house that served as a kitchen, for a chat with his
friends, the two merry men cooks. And as usual, he had
come away with a handful of cakes.

"Cakes! Cakes! Ah Shung is eating cakes!" the children
cried to each other, and they made a rush for the boy."

"These are mine," Ah Shung cried. "They are small!
Wang Lai will bring for you a great bowlful. She is even
now on her way." The boy was not really selfish. But he
could not help teasing his playmates a little. He ran away
from them, holding his cakes clutched tight in his hand.
Up this path, down that one, the children pursued him.

At last they trapped Ah Shung in the very middle of
the white humpbacked bridge that rose over the Pool of
the Goldfish. There was a playful scuffle. Then a shout
arose. The cakes had been knocked out of Ah Shung's

hand and had fallen in a shower of crumbs into the water. The red dragon-eyed goldfish snapped up the crumbs hungrily, almost before Ah Shung knew what had happened. His grandmother, who had been watching the little play, burst into a merry laugh at the change in the boy's face.

"The goldfish won in that battle!" she called out to him. "But do not feel badly, Small Bear; Wang Lai will come with the cakes for us all. You will just have to wait like the others. You only received the reward you deserved for being so stingy. It happened with you as with the stingy fruit peddler in the tale of the wonderful pear tree. Come, rest here beside me, and I will tell you about him."

"Long, long ago, on a summer afternoon when the sun shone as brightly as it does today, this stingy fruit peddler halted his wheelbarrow at the side of the road which ran between two large towns and upon which many people were always going and coming. He had tied an umbrella to the top of a pole so that it shaded his baskets of luscious brown pears. 'The day is hot. It is dusty,' he said to himself. 'Travelers will be thirsty. I shall sell every one of my ripe juicy pears.'

"All sorts of men passed the wheelbarrow of this fruit peddler. Some had money to buy pears, and went on their way licking their lips. Others could not spare even a few pennies. They could only look thirstily at the baskets on the wheelbarrow under the umbrella.

"In the midst of the afternoon there came along an old

man dressed like a farmer. He wore a blue jacket and blue trousers which were dusty and dirty, as though he had just finished his work. Over one shoulder he carried a hoe, and he looked very tired. His forehead had not been shaved for many days, and his untidy queue grew out of a little forest of bristles. He looked as though he had allowed the rains to wash his face and the winds to comb his hair for him.

"But if you had examined him closely, my children, you would have seen that there was something strange about this old man. His eyes were brighter and his face finer than those of the other farmers who passed along the crowded road. But the fruit peddler saw only that he was shabby and that he was too poor to buy his wares.

" 'O Worthy Fruit Peddler,' the old man said as he paused before the wheelbarrow, 'I am thirsty. I have no money to buy your pears, but I feel sure that you will be glad to spare one for a man of such a great age as mine.'

" 'Depart, Worthless Beggar,' the stingy fruit peddler cried. 'My pears are for sale. I do not give them away to every rascal who stops before my wheelbarrow.'

" 'I am old. My tongue is aching with thirst,' the aged farmer insisted. 'I do not ask for a fine pear. Give me the poorest, the smallest one, in your baskets, and I will call down blessings upon you.'

" 'Why should I need your blessings, Old Wretch? Get you gone before I beat you!' The fruit seller shouted so loud that the noise drew a crowd about his wheelbarrow.

" 'For shame, fruit peddler,' said a bystander, 'this farmer is old and weary. He is thirsty and poor. Give him a pear! One small pear will bring you but little money, and it will give him refreshment. You will be repaid by the satisfaction your kind action will give you.' The other bystanders echoed his plea, for they, too, felt pity for the tired, dusty old man.

" 'You are generous with my property,' the stingy fruit peddler cried angrily. 'I give no pears away. I should not gain satisfaction by such a foolish action. If you care so much for this old fool, why do you not give yourselves that satisfaction you speak of by buying a pear for him with your own money?' "

"The same bystander who had spoken first laid down a few copper coins and selected a large pear from the fruit peddler's basket. He put it into the hands of the thirsty old farmer, who received it with a bow and with polite words of thankfulness.

"So unusual was the appearance of the old farmer that the crowd lingered while he ate the ripe juicy pear down to the core. Then, to their surprise, he picked out all the seeds and turned them over and over in the palm of his hand. One of them he selected, and the others he threw away.

" 'You have been so kind to me, Honorable Gentlemen,' he said to the crowd, 'that I shall now show you something which you have perhaps never seen and which may amuse you.'

"Taking up the hoe which he had laid down by the road-side, the old man dug a hole in the earth. In this he placed the seed which he had chosen with such care. He scattered earth over it and pressed it down with his foot.

" 'For my little play I have need of a pot of hot water. Does any one here know where I might get such a thing?' he asked of the crowd, which by this time were much interested in his curious actions. One young man who was fond of a joke and who lived near by brought him a kettle from his own kitchen. The old farmer sprinkled the ground with the hot water, and, in less time than it takes to tell it, a tiny green shoot appeared in the earth where the seed had been planted.

"A few moments more and it was a pear tree almost a foot high. And as the crowd stood by, dumfounded, it grew and it grew, until it was as tall as the pear tree here in our garden. Before their very eyes buds appeared, the tree burst into bloom, the blossoms fell off, and the fruit formed. The little pears swelled and swelled. They grew brown and soft, and lo, they were ripe!

"By this time the crowd was so great that it blocked the highway. More and more people gathered as the news of the strange happening spread through the neighborhood.

" 'You young lads whose legs are more nimble than mine, climb up the tree,' the old farmer said. 'Pick the ripe fruit and hand it down to us thirsty ones.' The young men stripped the branches. Everyone in the crowd was given a pear. Even the stingy fruit peddler, who had left his wheelbarrow to watch, ate of the fruit from the wonderful pear tree.

"When the fruit had been eaten the old farmer raised his hoe and with two or three blows he cut down the pear tree. It fell to the ground and, as the crowd watched, its leaves seemed to shrivel and its branches grow smaller. At last the only part left was the slender tree trunk. The old farmer picked this up and, using it as a staff upon which to lean, he went on his way with a low bow to the crowd, who stood speechless with wonder. So quickly was it over that they would scarcely have believed it had happened if there had not remained in their hands the cores of the pears they had eaten.

"But hardly had the old farmer gone out of sight than there came a sharp scream from the stingy fruit peddler. 'My pears! My pears!' he cried. 'They have all disappeared. All my money spent for those pears and now they are gone! It was that wretch of a farmer. He must have been a fairy. Ai, ai, it was my pears he used to deck his wonderful tree.'

" 'If that is true,' said a bystander, 'the old man rewarded you well. You deserved nothing less for your treatment of him.' But the stingy fruit peddler did not hear. He was already running along down the road as hard as he could, in search of the old farmer."

"Did he find the old farmer, Lao Lao?" Yu Lang asked eagerly.

"No, Precious Pearl, he did not," replied her grandmother. "The only thing he found was the old farmer's staff, the trunk of the pear tree. And that staff, my children, was really the pole to which the fruit seller had tied his umbrella in order to shelter his fruit."

"And were the pears on the wonderful tree really those from the baskets of the stingy fruit peddler, Lao Lao?" Ah Shung asked curiously.

"How could I know that, Small Bear?" said Grandmother Ling. "But whether they were or whether they were not, the old man was surely a fairy who had taken the form of a farmer. Perhaps he had been sent just to give the stingy peddler a lesson in his duty to his fellows. The Jade Emperor of Heaven is kind. And to those who do not pity the poor and who do not have respect for the aged he is sure to send punishment of one sort or another."

"I think that fruit peddler must have given away a pear now and then after that lesson," Ah Shung said as he jumped down off the stone seat.

His grandmother smiled as she replied, "And I should think that Ah Shung must have learned that it's better to share his cakes with his cousins than to throw them all to the goldfish."

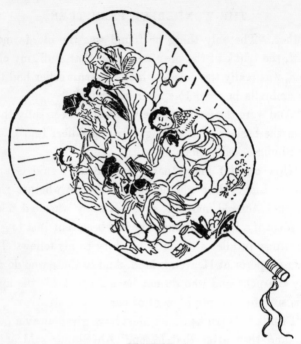

XVIII

HOW THE EIGHT OLD ONES CROSSED
THE SEA

Aᴛ ᴀʟᴍᴏsᴛ ᴇᴠᴇʀʏ ɢᴀᴛᴇ in the city there were new red
good-luck papers and, beside them, little bunches of
Indian grass whose sharp swordlike leaves would be sure
to frighten away the wicked spirits. Inside each sky-well
behind the red gate of the Lings there was hurry and
bustle, for it was the Fifth Day of the Fifth Moon, the

day for the Feast of the Dragon Boats, the holiday Ah
Shung and Yu Lang liked best of all holidays, except, of
course, the New Year.

The children found it hard to wait until it was time
to ride in the procession of little jinrikishas that went
from their red gate to the lake just outside the high city
wall. How exciting it was to be dressed in their very best
holiday suits! How fine their mother and their grandmother looked in their gowns of light-colored silks,
with their green jade earrings, and with flowers tucked
beside their smooth coils of hair! And what a fairy place
was the lake shore! Hundreds of fat boats, called "junks,"
with trimmings of gay flowers, were anchored among its
water lilies and lotus plants.

One of those fat flower-decked junks was the pleasure
boat of the Ling family, and it was from its deck that they
were to watch the dragon-boat races which were about to
begin.

"Here they come! Here they come! Here come the
dragon boats!" Ah Shung had spied several long narrow
boats whose curving ends were carved in the shape of
splendid dragons. Some thirty young men sat behind their
paddles, which stuck out on each side like the legs of a
centipede. One boatman sat astride the neck of each
dragon and waved a flag back and forth to show which
way to go.

As the first race began, shouts rose from the gay crowds
along the lake shore and from the eager watchers on the

anchored boats. Flags flew. Fans fluttered. Even the dignified gentlemen, in their elegant gowns and caps of dark silk, forgot to be calm and jumped up from their deck chairs to see who would win. Tied to a tall bamboo pole set up on a boat at the end of the course was a bundle of rich silk, the prize for that dragon boat which should be first to reach it.

Race after race, shouting and cheering. Cups of hot jasmine tea passed again and again to quench summer thirst, and a lunch which included small cone-shaped rice cakes wrapped in palm leaves filled the day with joy for Ah Shung and little Yu Lang. When the last dragon boat had reached the last goal, the people on shore sought the shade of the willow trees and made happy groups upon the grassy slopes. The Ling family lingered upon the deck of their boat. It was pleasant there in the path of the breeze which blew over the lake and cooled the hot summer day. And there was much to talk about—the speed of the dragon boats, friends who could be seen on the neighboring pleasure junks, and, above all, the good rains sure to be sent by the dragons who lived in the lake and who must have been pleased with the honor done their boats this day.

"Do you know, my children, how the dragon boats first came to be?" the Old Old One asked Ah Shung and Yu Lang, who were sitting on some cushions close to her chair on the deck of the pleasure junk.

"Tell us again, if you please, Lao Lao. I have forgotten," Yu Lang said, as she wiped the crumbs of a rice cake from her lips.

"It was long, long ago, when our country was still divided into different kingdoms," Grandmother Ling began. "In one of these kingdoms there lived a poet whose name was Chu Yuan. He was a court minister as well as a poet, and he helped rule the land. All was peaceful and happy under his guidance, and everyone loved him. But also in this kingdom there lived another minister who was as wicked and greedy as Chu Yuan was good and unselfish. He flattered the king, and, little by little, he turned him away from the path of good works down which Chu Yuan had led him. They spent money like water, did the king and his greedy minister, and they sowed seeds of unhappiness among the people.

"Chu Yuan begged the king to give up his evil ways, but he would not listen. At last, in despair, the good poet decided to throw himself into the river. 'Perhaps then,' he said, 'the king will be sorry and will come to his senses.'

"When the people heard that Chu Yuan had jumped into the river they wept. They set out in boats to look for him. They searched and they searched, but the river was deep and no trace could be found. They made up packets of food which they threw into the river lest he should be hungry. But one of the officials saw Chu Yuan in a dream. 'I cannot get the food you send,' the poet seemed to say. 'It melts in the water! Wrap it in palm leaves so that it will keep dry.' And that, my children, is why on this day of the year we always roll up our steamed rice cakes in tender green leaves and tie them with palm fibers.

"Ever since that time when the people searched for Chu Yuan, on this Fifth Day of the Fifth Moon, boats fill the lakes and the rivers in memory of the good poet. When it rains on this day we know that the gods in the sky also weep for Chu Yuan."

"But why couldn't they find Chu Yuan, Lao Lao?" asked Ah Shung.

"Who knows, Little Bear?" the Old Old One replied. "Perhaps he was hidden in the Dragon King's palace. They needed the magic gourd which Old Li used at the time when the Eight Old Ones crossed the sea. With it they could have seen the bottom of the river, no matter how deep it was, and they would surely have discovered Chu Yuan, just as the Old Ones found their lost comrade."

The children knew well the Eight Old Ones of whom their grandmother spoke. Upon vases in the family hall, on some of the teapots and the eating bowls, on fans, and on scroll paintings they had seen likenesses of these eight famous persons who possessed the gift of living forever, and who usually traveled together.

There was Old Li, with his iron crutch and his great gourd into which he jumped each night in order to sleep. There was Chung Li, who always carried a fine feather fan to show he had been an important official. And there was Old Chang on his white mule. The story said Chang's white mule was made out of paper and that when he did not need it he folded it up and put it away in his pocket. When he wished to travel again he had only to breathe on the paper steed and it was ready to carry him for thousands of miles. Sometimes Chang was painted riding with his face to the tail of his mule; sometimes, with it turned toward the mule's ears; and in his hand he held a rosy peach or a long phoenix feather.

Ah Shung liked Old Lu, with the magic sword which had been given him by the fire dragon and which helped him to hide in the Heavenly Kingdom, while Yu Lang's favorite Old Ones were Han, with his flower basket, who had made such strange plants to grow, and Ho, with her lotus blossom and peach-of-long-life. Ho was the only woman among the famous Eight Old Ones. The little girl was interested, too, in Lan, the Old One with the flute. She herself was learning to play tunes on a "pi-pa," an instrument with four strings, which in other lands is known as a lute. The most elegant of all the Old Ones, the children thought, was Tsao, who never forgot his wood tablet which showed he belonged to the Emperor's family.

These Eight Old Ones always seemed calm and happy. There were smiles on their painted faces. Because they were sure of living forever, their number, "eight," was said to be lucky.

"I thought the Eight Old Ones always traveled on clouds, Lao Lao," said Ah Shung when his grandmother spoke of their crossing the sea.

"Perhaps they were tired of riding back and forth through the sky. Perhaps they thought they should like to see the realm of the Dragon King under the sea," the old woman replied. "For one day they did come down from the clouds and set forth over the waters. A picture I have at home shows them in a boat, but the story says that they each rode by themselves, Li on his iron crutch, Chung on his fan, Chang on his white mule, and Lu on his sword. Han sat on his flower basket, and Ho in the heart of her lotus blossom, while Lan's boat was his flute, and Tsao's his wooden tablet.

"In these curious ways the Eight Old Ones traveled upon the sea safely, until the Dragon King's son, looking up from below, saw the flute of Old Lan. This Dragon Prince gave his father much trouble, for he was always forgetting the rules of behavior. This time he decided that he wanted that flute for himself, so he seized poor Old Lan and made him his prisoner under the sea.

"The Old Ones were alarmed when they found that Lan and his flute had disappeared under the waves. And it was then that Old Li brought forth his magic gourd. He turned its mouth downward toward the sea bottom, and at once there streamed forth such a strong light that every cranny and corner of the Dragon King's realm was as bright as the day.

"On the floor of the ocean the Old Ones could see the splendid palaces of colored stone through which the light shone. They could catch the shimmer of the Dragon King's pearls and the fiery lights from his opals. Before their eyes the fish swimming in the very deepest parts of the sea were as plain as the goldfish are to us out in our garden.

"But the Dragon King was alarmed at the strong beam of light that disturbed his dim kingdom, and he sent a messenger to find out whence it had come.

" 'The Dragon King's peace is destroyed by that bright light,' the messenger said to the Old Ones. 'He bids you turn it away.'

" 'Say to the Dragon King,' the Old Ones replied, 'that we seek for our comrade, Lan, and his flute. The Dragon Prince seized him. We can see that he is a prisoner down there in his palace.'

"When the messenger returned the Dragon King called his wicked son to him and he bade him give up Old Lan and his flute. But the prince refused to obey, and he set forth with his sword to attack the Old Ones who had dared send such a message to the Dragon King. As he drew near the Old Ones they let down a line with a great fishing hook on it. They caught the wicked prince and made him their prisoner. 'Tell the Dragon King,' they said, 'that we will restore his son to him when he has set our comrade free.'

"The Dragon King was reasonable. He knew his son had done wrong, and he was about to let Old Lan go free, when his court ministers objected. 'Who are these, mighty Dragon King,' they said, 'that they should dare to hold our prince prisoner just because of a flute and one aged man? Permit us to give them a taste of our power.'

"The court ministers insisted, until at last the Dragon King consented that the undersea armies should be sent forth to find the Old Ones who held the Dragon Prince prisoner. In the meantime these Old Ones had called upon all the men who, like themselves, had the power of living forever. They called on the gods in the Heavenly Kingdom and on the spirits who dwell on the mountains of Kun Lun in the realm of the Western Empress.

"What a battle there was when the two mighty armies came face to face with each other. The noise was so great that it woke the god who rules all the waters, and he came forth from his palace to see what it meant. When he heard the story he was angry with the Dragon King and his son, and he threatened to take their kingdom away.

" 'Give back the flute and set free its owner,' the Water God ordered, 'and see that you make welcome to your kingdom those Eight Blessed Old Ones.'

"Well, the Dragon Prince was surly, but he made no more trouble, and the Dragon King opened up the waters so that the Eight Old Ones might explore his undersea realm. All the things they saw there and the adventures they had would take too long to tell, my children. The sky dragons have already drawn the sun's chariot to the edge of the world and it is time for us to go home."

XIX

THE WHITE SNAKE

I SHALL EAT the spider," Ah Shung said to his sister.

"I shall eat the toad," the little girl replied, as she chose a cake from the plate which a maid set on the table.

The Ling family was gathered for the evening meal in the family hall. After their long day at the dragon-boat races everyone was tired. The Old Old One made no move to rise from her seat at the head of the red-covered table, even though the last bowl of rice had long since been emptied.

"Mine is a centipede," and "Mine is a scorpion," two of the other children cried as they examined the sugar on the cakes they had selected. These cakes with the likenesses of insects and animals on their round tops were always served at the Ling tables on this Fifth Day of the Fifth Moon.

"And I have a snake," Lao Lao called across to the children, whose excited voices she had overheard. "All the five poisonous creatures are here. It is well that we pay heed to them, for this is the day when they and their brothers crawl out of their holes. I trust Wang Lai has given each one of you the drink that keeps them away. We must take care, or trouble might come to us on this account, as it came on this day so long ago when the White Snake brought the flood."

"We do not quite understand those words, Lao Lao," Ah Shung said as his grandmother finished the last bite of her cake. "Please tell us what they mean." With the other children, the boy left his place at the smaller table and crossed the great room to his grandmother's side.

"It is a story, Small Bear," the Old Old One said, "but it is not a long story, and if you are not too weary after your journey to the lake, I will tell it to you. One day, hundreds of years ago, a young man, whom we may as well call Ming, was walking along between the rice fields outside the town where he lived. In the distance he saw a crowd of young men, shouting and laughing and jumping about.

"Ming hurried to find out what they were doing, and when he had pushed his way through the group, he saw on the ground a snake as pale as white jade. The youths were tormenting it. They poked its coils with their staffs and they threw stones at its head. Almost they had killed it when the young man arrived.

"Now this lad had a kind heart. He could not bear to see anything suffer, not even a snake. He cried out to the young men who were worrying the poor creature and he bade them stop with such fierce words that they obeyed. When they had gone on their way, Ming brought the snake food to eat and water to drink.

"As Ming stood looking down at the white serpent, a strange thing happened, my loves. The creature began to writhe and to wriggle. All at once its snake's body disappeared and in its place there was a maiden so fair that Ming thought she must have flown down from the Heavenly Kingdom.

" 'To reward your kind heart, O Noble Young Man,' the fair maiden said, 'I will wed you, and good luck shall dwell with us under your roof.' Ming by no means objected to marrying such a beautiful girl, and he gladly took her home with him to his family courts.

"The young man and his bride were happy together. Ming had no idea that there was anything wrong until one day he climbed the mountain near by on whose top there stood a temple to the great god, Buddha. There, saying his prayers, Ming found an old monk whose head was shaved bare as a pumpkin and whose long robe was yellow, the color of mustard.

" 'Take care, young man,' the monk warned Ming. 'Take care! There is danger inside your gate.'

" 'How can that be, Holy Man?' Ming said, 'Inside our gate there are only my father and my mother and my dear wife.'

" 'But your wife is no ordinary wife, Good Young Sir,' the old monk replied, shaking his shaven head. 'She is a fairy. Whether she be a good fairy or a bad fairy, I do not know. But my advice to you is to stay hidden here in our temple out of her reach.'

"Ming was badly frightened. He remembered the white snake and how it had vanished just before his bride appeared. So he consented to take shelter with the yellow-robed monk.

"The young wife waited and waited for her husband to return. As the days and nights passed and he did not come back, she grew more and more angry. For, my children, it was indeed true that she was a fairy, the very white serpent which Ming had saved and which had the power of changing itself into a woman.

" 'I will find out where my husband is,' the White Snake said to herself. 'I will send a great flood to cover the land. That will surely drive him forth from the place where he is hiding.' And she changed herself into a white serpent again and darted out of the house. Across the fields she twisted and turned until she came to the lake, and it was her magic power that caused its water to rise and flow over the banks.

"The people rushed from their houses and sought safety on the hills. Up, up, rose the flood waters. They spread over the countryside like a vast sea. Soon no land could be seen but the top of the mountain. The old monk spread his yellow robe out as far as it would go, and such is the greatness of the god Buddha, my small ones, that it covered the entire peak.

"When the White Snake's flood reached the edge of the monk's robe, its waters stopped short. For her power was as nothing against the power of Buddha. When the fairy saw that her husband did not come forth from his hiding place and that the waters would go no further, she knew that her plan had failed. She sent the waters back into the lake and she changed her snake's body into that of a woman once more. Under a willow tree she sat down to weep and to wait until her husband should return of his own accord.

"In the temple on the mountain top the old monk spoke to Ming. 'One seeing is worth one hundred tellings,' he said, 'and you have seen for yourself the trouble your fairy wife has caused. But I have looked into the future and I find it is safe now for you to go back to your own home. In a short time your wife will present you with a son. He will be a wonderful child, for the spirit that will dwell in his body will be that of a god from the Heavenly Kingdom. Through him, honor and fame will come to your house.

" 'With this child,' the monk continued, 'your wife wipes out many of her sins of the past, but she cannot escape being punished for her wrongdoing in bringing the flood. No one, not even a fairy, can so go against the will of the gods.'

" 'O-yo, my poor wife,' Ming cried in despair. 'What is to become of her?'

" 'Do not fear, Good Young Man,' said the old monk. 'Your wife will not suffer. But she must spend the rest of her days beneath a pagoda, where she may prepare herself for the life-that-lasts-forever on the mountains of Kun Lun. Shut up so she will have no chance of raising the waters again.'

"And that is what happened to the White Snake, my children," Grandmother Ling said in ending her story. "A splendid pagoda, with five curving roofs, rose over her dwelling place under the earth. It was none other than the Thunder Peak Pagoda which still stands today near the West Lake and which some call the Pagoda of the White Snake. Inside it are kept the writings of the wise ones who set down the words of Buddha himself, and to it there go every year hundreds of scholars who wish to consult them."

"What happened to the baby that was born to the White Snake, Lao Lao?" asked Yu Lang.

"As the old monk foretold, Little Jade Flower," the Old Old One replied, "he was truly from heaven. He was wise. He was clever with the hair pen. Such splendid writings came from his hand that it was said he had to help him twelve tiny dragons, the messengers of the Black Pine whose oil helped make his ink. They lived in the well of his ink stone and they put such magic power into his ink that it was called Dragon Fragrance. It is because of this that we now often say of a poet, 'he has dipped his hair pen into the Dragon Fragrance.' And it is the son of the White Snake that we worship in these times as the God of Writings and Books."

XX

PRINCE CHU TI'S CITY

Sᴛʀᴀɴɢᴇʀꜱ ꜱɪᴛ ᴛᴏᴅᴀʏ with our father in the Hall of Politeness, Lao Lao," said Ah Shung when he came with Yu Lang for their afternoon visit in the Old Old One's apartment.

"I know," replied Grandmother Ling. "They are great men from Peking. I should like to hear the news they bring, but today I am tired and must rest." The old woman was half sitting, half lying, under a green silken comforter upon the broad brick bed. Its curtains were pushed back so that she could look out of her open window at the sunny courtyard and watch the goings and comings of her household.

"Ai, Peking, where the Emperor lives, is a great city," Lao Lao said to the children. "I have been there. I have walked on the top of the mighty wall that surrounds it. And what a sight I saw from that high place! Roofs, roofs, roofs, and among them the tops of the trees in the gardens! Across the sea of their gray tiles I could pick out the wall which surrounds the part of Peking that is called the Imperial City. There lie the courts of the most important mandarins, those fortunate men who hold high positions under the Emperor.

"I could even see the yellow-tiled roofs of the palaces of the Son of Heaven himself and pick out the high wall of pink brick that shuts them away from the rest of the world. The Emperor's courts are so many that they seem like a city. No one but princes and nobles may enter them. That is why, my little ones, the part of Peking where the Emperor dwells is called the Forbidden City."

"Did the Son of Heaven build Peking, Lao Lao?" Ah Shung asked.

"Not that one who now sits upon the Dragon Throne, Little Bear," was the reply. "How the present city of Peking was built is a long tale. But it is a good tale. I heard it from the lips of my own grandmother. Listen and I will tell it to you.

"Long, long ago the place of the Dragon Throne was in the city of Nanking, far to the southeast of our northern capital, Peking. There, in splendid palaces, the Emperor lived with his nobles about him. And thither from all parts of the land men journeyed to make their kowtows before him.

"The Son of Heaven of that time had several wives and the gods sent him many sons. It is not at all strange that the royal mothers should have been jealous of one another. Each was eager that her son should be chosen to take his father's place upon the Dragon Throne when the flower of the Emperor's life should have been plucked by the gods.

"The number one wife, the Empress herself, was more jealous than the rest. And this was strange because her son was the one whom the Emperor would have been most likely to choose. But as she saw the other princes grow up, she feared lest their father might take a strong fancy to this one or that one and put him in the place of her beloved son.

"Now, the Emperor was very fond of the Empress, and when she urged him to send the princes away he gave his consent. This one was made governor of a state to the west. That one was sent to rule over a state to the south, and others were kept away from the court on one pretext or another.

"The fourth son of the Emperor was a young man called Chu Ti. He was handsome and strong and pleasant of manner. Everyone in the palaces loved him above all the other princes, and the Emperor himself showed great affection for him.

" 'Your son, Chu Ti, is grown,' the Empress said to the Emperor one day. 'He is a splendid young man and you should give him a splendid state to rule over. That land of Yen to the north is now without a governor. Why do you not name your Chu Ti as Prince of Yen?'

" 'But the land of Yen is far. Even I do not know what sort of place it may be,' the Emperor said.

" 'All parts of the empire of Your Shining Majesty are glorious,' the wily Empress replied. 'Why should Yen be an exception? It is the very place for Chu Ti.' And the Empress flattered her husband and begged him so hard that at last he gave in.

"When the good prince was ready to set forth on his long journey into the north, an old priest who loved him thrust into his hand a little sealed packet. 'Take this, my son,' said the old priest. 'Do not break its seal until you are in trouble. But when the time comes that you cannot see your way clearly, then open the packet and you may find help inside it.'

"Ai, my children, the wicked Empress well knew to what sort of a land she was sending poor Prince Chu Ti. Yen was a rough country. It had no fine cities. Its people were many but their houses had been destroyed by foes from the north. Chu Ti's heart was heavy when he saw his poor kingdom. He wept bitter tears and nothing his companions could say brought smiles to his face.

" 'Now indeed I am in trouble,' he said to himself. 'I do not know what to do. Surely this is the time to open the packet the kind old priest gave me.' So he broke its seal. Inside there were a number of thin folded papers. He took out the first, unfolded it, and read: 'When you come to the land of Yen, you, Chu Ti, must build a magnificent city. Summon your friends to aid you and lay out your building after this plan.' Upon the priest's paper was traced the map of a city more splendid than Chu Ti ever had dreamed of. He called his companions about him and he told of the great city which he wished to build. Many among them were rich. They so loved the good prince that they were happy to lay their wealth at his feet, and they sent for their friends of other rich families to help him also.

"The news of the city that Chu Ti was to build spread over the land, and hundreds of thousands of men came to the north. Each step of the way Chu Ti followed the directions in the priest's little packet. White stones were brought from the wild hills to the west. Great bricks were made from clay in the neighborhood, and a huge double wall was set up round the city. Earth dug from the moat was packed hard inside this so that the palaces it enclosed should be safe from all robbers. Nine gates under tall towers each with three curving roofs were let into the wall.

"In the heart of Chu Ti's city splendid temples were built to honor the gods of heaven and earth, and outside its wall a mountain of coal was laid up for use in time of war. I myself saw 'Coal Hill,' my children, with its five peaks upon which five temples are built. Its sides are now covered with grass, but it is well known that there is a store of coal underneath.

"And the palaces Chu Ti built! Of the whitest of marble, with dragons carved in their stones, they were far more magnificent than those of his father, the Emperor, in Nanking. Each curving roof was covered with tiles of the Emperor's own color, yellow, and on their ridges little yellow porcelain lions and dragons stood guard against evil spirits. There were gardens and lakes, deep wells and tanks, and about the high wall was a moat filled with water upon which lilies floated.

"The good prince was so pleased with his splendid city that he called before him all the friends who had given him aid. 'From this day,' he declared, 'as a mark of my gratitude, you and your children shall have the right to embroider on the cuffs of your robes our imperial dragon.' And from that day to this, my dear ones, when a man has been granted great favors we say 'he has received the dragon cuff.'

"The fame of Prince Chu Ti's city grew and grew. From every part of the empire came merchants with their most costly wares. Fine shops were built. Courtyards were laid out for family dwellings. There was plenty and peace.

Nowhere in the empire was there a state so pleasant to live in as that land of Yen.

"But there are dark days and bright days in every moon, my heart's treasures," the Old Old One said, shaking her head. "And so there came a time when the brightness of Chu Ti's city was darkened. For one morning his ministers came before him, wringing their hands. 'The wells are thirsty,' they wailed. 'The rivers are dry. The people are fearful.'

"Prince Chu Ti called upon the court fortune teller and asked him the reason why the water had gone out from the wells and the rivers.

"'I see it all clearly,' said the wise fortune teller as soon as he had gazed at the stars and peered into his books. 'When you dug the foundation for the east wall of the city you broke into the cave of a dragon who had lived there for thousands of years. That dragon was angry and wished to depart. But his dragon wife protested, 'Why should we leave our home where we have dwelt in peace for so long? Let us rather drive out the Prince of Yen. Let us take all his water. Then his people will go and leave us alone.'

"'O-yo,' the prince exclaimed, 'perhaps the dream I had last night will throw more light upon that. In my sleep it seemed that an old man and an old woman knelt down before me. They begged to be permitted to go away from my city and they asked to be allowed to take along with them two baskets of water. I gave them permission. What can it mean?'

"And since the prince was in deep trouble and could not see his way clearly, he took out again the precious sealed packet which the old priest had given him. He drew out another paper. And upon it he read: 'The old man and the old woman whom you saw in your dream are the dragons who live in the cave outside the east wall. In those magic baskets of theirs they are carrying off all the waters of Peking. Make haste to pursue them.'

"With his spear in his hand, on the fastest horse in his stables, Prince Chu Ti galloped after the water thieves. And soon he came upon the very old man and his wife whom he had seen in his dream. They were dragging a cart with the two baskets of water loaded upon it. Without warning them Chu Ti thrust his spear into one of the baskets. Then he galloped away to a high hill, as the priest's writing had told him to do. From the hole he made in the basket a huge stream of water gushed forth over the land. In less time than it takes me to tell it, it covered the country like a mighty lake. It surrounded the hilltop where Prince Chu Ti stood, so that it seemed like an island.

" 'Do not be alarmed, dear Chu Ti, I will call on heaven to help you,' said a voice that came from behind him. And Chu Ti, turning round, saw to his amazement that it was his old friend, the priest. No sooner had the priest said a prayer than the waters began to fall back, and they returned to their places in the rivers and wells.

"Nothing was seen of the old man and his wife, but the

broken basket became a hole in the earth so large that you could drop a temple inside it. From its bottom a huge stream of clear water spurted up like a fountain. And in its very center Prince Chu Ti saw a tall tower with many curving roofs set one over the other. It was a pagoda which rested upon the top of the fountain, just as boats float on our lake. Up and down it went as the waters rose and fell, and sometimes its tip disappeared in the clouds, so high leaped the fountain.

"Today that pagoda no longer rests on the water. It stands on a hill at the foot of which is the spring from which water is carried to make the tea for the Son of Heaven in the Forbidden City. Men often call it The-Pagoda-That-Holds-the-Waters-in-Place. And they say that since the Prince of Yen outwitted the two dragons his city of Peking has never lacked water in its rivers and wells."

XXI

KO-AI'S LOST SHOE

Tell us more about Peking, Lao Lao," Yu Lang begged when her grandmother had finished the tale about the beginnings of the northern capital of their great land.

"With so many words, my tongue is as thirsty as the wells of Chu Ti," the old woman said. "Bid Huang Ying bring tea, and then you shall hear about the great bell I saw when I went to Peking."

Water was always boiling and ready to be poured over dried leaves in the little tea bowls. The water in the Ling wells, as in all the wells in the city, was not good to drink. "Drink water unboiled, or throw yourself in the river. It is all the same," old Wang Lai, the nurse, used to tell the children. So when they were thirsty the Lings always drank this steaming hot water flavored with fragrant tea.

"Ai, my children, this gives strength," the Old Old One said, as she daintily sipped her cup of hot tea. With her forefinger she held its little saucer-like cover so as to push back the tea leaves that floated on top of the pale green-yellow liquid. She drank her tea noisily because she thought that showed how much she enjoyed it.

"Now you shall hear the tale of the great bell of Peking and how poor Ko-Ai lost her shoe," the Old Old One said. "There are two mighty towers that rise high over the walls of the northern capital. One is the tower upon which stands the great drum that gives the time for the whole city. Here in our courtyard, Fu, who makes our time-sticks, sets them by the sun and stars. You have seen how he covers a stick with clay and burning-powder. You know how he marks it in even sections that take just so long to burn. It is our time-stick that tells us whether it is the hour of the dragon or the hour of the monkey.

"But in the Drum Tower of Peking there is a water clock that measures the twelve hours of the day. By means of it the keeper of the drum can tell when to strike the hour of the rat, the hour of the tiger, and all the other hours into which our day is divided. Blows on the drum boom over the city, and everyone sets his time-sticks by its thunder.

"When night comes and it is the hour for people to close their gates tight, the great bell in the other tall tower is rung. So huge is it and so loud its tone that its clear voice is heard in every courtyard. 'Boom-m-m-m' goes the bell, and then if you listen you can hear a note that sounds like 'shieh-h-h-h,' which people say is the whispering wail of the lovely Ko-Ai, calling for her lost shoe.

"It all happened long ago when the Emperor Yung Lo sat on the Dragon Throne in Peking. His workmen had laid up great bricks and stones into two mighty towers which stand there today. They had built them high and they had built them huge, so that they should be the most splendid watchtowers in all the land.

" 'We shall place a great drum upon one, and we must have a bell for the other to warn the whole city when foes draw near,' the Emperor said. 'It must be such a bell as has never before been heard. Mixed with its iron it must have in it brass to make its tones strong, gold to make its tones rich, and silver to make its tones sweet. And we must be able to hear it for a distance as long as that of the wall that surrounds all Peking.'

"Well, the metals were brought from the mines deep in the earth, and bellmakers were summoned from all parts of the empire. They labored for many days, and at last the mixed metal was ready for pouring into the bell mold. The fortune teller consulted the stars and set a lucky day, upon which the Emperor and his court assembled to watch the great bell being cast. The court musicians played while the hot melted metal was poured into the mold. Then the Emperor and his attendants departed, leaving Kuan Yu, the master bellmaker, to watch the mold cool.

"Ai-yah, my little ones, that day was not lucky, in spite of the fortune teller. For as soon as Kuan Yu took the bell from the mold he saw that the metal was as full of fine holes as a honeycomb.

"The Emperor was vexed, for much time and money had been spent in making the bell. But he gave Kuan Yu the order to try once again. More metal was brought in from the mines, and more care than before was taken with mixing it. Again, when the mold was ready and the metal was melted, the Emperor and his court gathered about it. But again, when his bell cooled, the unlucky bellmaker found the same holes in its sides.

"This time the Emperor was angry indeed. He called Kuan Yu to him and said, 'Once more, O Bellmaker, I give you a chance. But if you fail now, your head shall come off.'

"Poor Kuan Yu was filled with terror. He returned to his home with dismay written upon his face, and even the efforts of his beloved daughter, Ko-Ai, failed to pierce his deep gloom. Ko-Ai was a maiden about sixteen years old. She was the only child of the bellmaker, and he loved her as his life. She was beautiful as the new moon, with eyes shaped like an almond and brows curved like a willow leaf.

Her skin was white as rice and her hair black as lacquer. Not too tall nor too short, when she walked she swayed to and fro like a flower in the spring breeze. Ko-Ai could make verses as well as a poet, and her embroidery was as fine as the best needlework in the empire. She never forgot her duty to her father and mother, and she kept all the rules for maidenly conduct.

"Kuan Yu, the bellmaker, went about his task of making this third bell with a heavy heart. He watched each step of mixing the metals himself. He took every precaution, but still he could not be sure that his bell would be perfect.

"The good and lovely Ko-Ai could think of nothing but her poor father and the sad fate that awaited him if he should fail. One day she secretly asked advice from a fortune teller, who replied to her thus:

> *"Gold and iron will not wed,*
> *Nor brass and silver share a bed,*
> *Unless with maiden's blood they're blended*
> *Your father's life will soon be ended.*

"The maiden trembled at the words of the soothsayer. 'What other maiden save Ko-Ai would there be?' she asked herself. But such was her love for her dear father that she felt no price too great to pay for his life. Without telling him what she had in her mind, Ko-Ai begged Kuan Yu that she might be present when the third bell was molded.

"For a third time, when the metal was melted in the great caldron, the Emperor and his princes gathered and the court musicians played. Then, just as the rushing stream of hot metal flowed into the mold the bellmaker's daughter, the lovely Ko-Ai, said in a low voice, 'It is for thee, O my father.' And she rushed to the side of the bell mold and threw herself into the stream. The metal bubbled up in a fountain of bright colors and then it flowed smoothly, filling the mold. Everyone cried out. They rushed to the side of the bell mold. But there was nothing to be seen of Ko-Ai except one tiny shoe which remained in the hand of her old nurse, who had tried to catch hold of her as she jumped.

"But the soothsayer had spoken truly, for when the great bell was rung, it was as the Emperor had wished, more perfect and more powerful than any bell upon earth. Its boom could be heard across the whole city. And when it was struck, after each great note there was a whispering wail that sounded like 'shieh-h-h.' I myself have heard it. Who knows, that whisper may indeed be Ko-Ai calling and calling for her lost shoe, as people say. Though I feel certain her spirit is happy. So good a daughter as she has surely been well rewarded by the Jade Emperor of Heaven.

"Another tale is told about that great bell in Peking, my children," Grandmother Ling added. "Men say that if it is struck by a strange hand, rain falls from the sky. Upon the day I stood near it, a party of sharp-nosed foreigners from over the sea came to visit the bell. They looked at it with their round muddy eyes and one wished to strike it. The bellkeeper told them that the sky dragons would be angry and that they would send rain. But the ignorant strangers would not believe it.

"I think they must have paid the bellkeeper well, for at last he permitted them to draw back the great wooden beam and to drive it against the side of the bell. The noise made me deaf for the rest of the day, so loud was its tone. But hardly had the notes of the great bell died away than the black clouds that formed overhead were split with sharp lightning. Thunder rolled and the rain fell upon us in torrents. The guards laughed at the surprise of the fuzzy-haired foreigners. But so stupid were they that, even then, they would not believe that it was ringing the bell that had brought on the storm."

XXII

THE SPINNING MAID AND THE COWHERD

O<small>FTEN</small> on hot summer evenings the Lings, big and little, gathered about the round stone table in their Garden of Sweet Smells. There under the star-sprinkled sky the air was cooler than in the family hall or in the apartment of the Old Old One. In the soft moonlight fans could be seen moving forward and back. The leaves of the trees rustled and the distant wind bells tinkled faintly now and then in the light breeze. The children sat silent upon the curving stone benches, listening to the poems and the stories which their elders recited.

"The Silver River is clear and calm tonight," said Grandmother Ling as she looked up at the broad streak of white light made by the stars in the Milky Way. "It is well. The poor Spinning Maid will be able to cross safely the Bridge of the Magpies when she goes to meet her beloved Cowherd tonight."

Everyone around the stone table understood what Grandmother Ling meant. Ah Shung and Yu Lang knew by heart this tale of the Spinning Maid and the Cowherd. They had heard it again only that morning, as they had every Seventh Day of every Seventh Moon since they were born.

As the Old Old One told the story, one day long, long ago a handsome young man was tending his water cow by the side of a stream. He was fond of the huge black beast that drew his plow for him, and he took care to lead her where the greenest grass grew and where there was water deep enough for her to wallow to her heart's content.

As the youth lay on the grassy bank beside the grazing cow, he saw seven maidens swimming about in the river, and he was startled, for they were more beautiful than any maidens he had ever seen, even in dreams. Now his water cow was a fairy beast which had the power of talking, and, as the young man looked in wonder at the seven fair maids, words came from her mouth.

"Those are maidens from the Heavenly Kingdom, kind

Only the seventh, the fair spinning maid could not find her red robe and was forced to stay behind

Cowherd," the water cow said. "The six who swim there in a group are well enough, but the seventh, that one by herself on the other side of the stream, is the fairest and the wisest of them all. In her palace in heaven she has a spinning wheel and a loom upon which she spins thread and makes cloth for the gods. Such fine silk she makes! It is softer than the softest cloud and its colors are those of the most brilliant sunset.

"It is because of your goodness to me, master," the water cow added, "that I tell you the secret of this Spinning Maid. You must hide her red robe, that one by yonder stone. Without it she cannot fly back to the sky. She will have to remain here on the earth and you may be able to marry her."

The Cowherd did as the animal bade him, and when the seven fair maids had finished their swimming, six put on their robes and rode away to the sky on the backs of white cranes. Only the seventh, the fair Spinning Maid, could not find her red robe and was forced to stay behind. But the Spinning Maid was not unhappy. She found the young Cowherd so handsome, so kind, and so good that she gladly consented to remain on earth as his wife. And they lived together as sweetly as two doves in a nest.

For three years nothing happened to disturb them. Two beautiful children brought light to their household, and under their roof love and joy reigned. But in the Heavenly Kingdom no soft silken garments came from the loom which the Spinning Maid left behind her. None of her sisters could spin such fine silk nor weave such smooth cloth.

When the Empress of Heaven discovered this fact she sent a messenger to earth to bid the Spinning Maid return to her sky loom, and one day the cowherd came home from the fields to find his wife gone. He was sad and he wept, and as he tended his water cow he told her his troubles.

"Do not be sad, O my kind master," the water cow said. "My end is near. In a few days my spirit will go to the Shadowy World. When that time comes, you must strip off my hide and wrap yourself in it. Then I myself will take you to join your dear Spinning Maid up in the sky."

It happened just so. Hardly had the Cowherd wrapped himself in the hide than he felt himself rising into the air. Up, up, up, he went, and he did not stop until he had come to the palace of his dear wife, the Spinning Maid.

How happy they were to be together again! The Spinning Maid was so glad to see her Cowherd that she forgot all about her spinning wheel and her loom. For days they lay idle, and when the Empress of Heaven saw this she again became angry. With her silver hairpin she drew a line across the sky, which straightway became the River of Stars that cuts the heavens in two.

The Lings believed that the Silver River flowed down from the sky onto the earth, where it became the muddy stream called the Huang Ho. This name means Yellow River. The Old Old One explained that the silver color of the heavenly stream turned to yellow as soon as it touched the ground.

"Since the Spinning Maid cannot keep to her loom when the Cowherd is with her, they must dwell apart. She shall live on one side, he on the other side, of this Heavenly River," the angry Empress declared. And she changed the Spinning Maid and her husband into two twinkling stars. Grandmother Ling often showed the children the Spinning Maid's star on one side of the Silver River and on the other side, across the band of white light, the star of the Cowherd. She also pointed out two tiny stars not far away which she said might be their two children.

After they had been so cruelly parted, tears never ceased falling from the eyes of the Spinning Maid and smiles never came to the face of the good Cowherd. The Emperor of Heaven was sad at the sight of such great unhappiness and he decided to help them.

"It can do no harm for these lovers to meet once a year," he said to the Empress. "On each Seventh Day of each Seventh Moon let them come together once more."

Reluctantly the Empress gave her consent. But she provided no bridge by which the Spinning Maid might cross the broad silver stream. It was the kind magpies from the earth who took pity upon her. They gathered together from all parts of the world and flew up to the sky. Each bird grasped the feathers of one of the others in his strong beak. The magpies packed themselves so tightly together that they made a bridge quite strong enough to bear the weight of the Spinning Maid as she ran across to the Cowherd.

Ah Shung and Yu Lang would have been surprised indeed to find a magpie in their garden on the Seventh Day of the Seventh Moon. They were always sure that by midday these noisy birds had flown up to heaven to make their bridge. Perhaps it was because this kind deed of the magpie brought such happiness to the Heavenly Lovers that in China such birds are called "birds of joy," and that their singing is a sign of good luck to come.

Yu Lang had been taught to say, on this day each year, a little prayer for fair weather. Her grandmother explained that if it should rain the Silver River would rise and wash away the bridge of birds. Then the Spinning Maid would have to wait for twelve long moons more before she could see her beloved Cowherd.

The women inside the red gate of the Lings always celebrated the day of the Spinning Maid. They considered her the Goddess of Weaving, and they looked to her for help in making smooth silk cloth on their looms and in setting fine stitches in their embroideries. The women and girls of the family set bowls of water out in the courtyard where the sun could shine full upon it. In these little bowls tiny needles, light as a feather, floated on top of the clear water. Exactly at midday the women peered anxiously into their bowls. By the shapes of the shadows cast by their needles they told their own fortunes, and they thought in this way they could find out whether they would have good luck with their needlework during the year.

The girls also had searched their courtyard for spider

webs. They were delighted when they found a perfect one outside one of their windows, for they thought it a sign that they would do well with their handiwork.

"The feast we have made tonight for the Spinning Maid is a poor thing compared with those during the reigns of the ancient Emperors," said the Old Old One. "I have been reading how one Empress had towers covered with silk, a thousand feet high, built up toward the heavens. On top of these silken towers fair maidens played lutes and sang for the pleasure of the Heavenly Lovers. And in the moonlight they held contests to see which of the princesses could most quickly thread needles, each of which had nine eyes."

"Our moon is bright. May we not try a needle contest ourselves, Lao Lao?" asked Ah Shung's older sister who prided herself on her skill in embroidery. The Old Mistress sent her maid to bring needles and thread. Each woman and each girl, even little Yu Lang, held her needle in one hand and her thread in the other. There was much merriment as they tried to put the silk through the needle eyes in the dim light of the night. Everyone shouted and clapped when Yu Lang held her threaded needle out before all the rest.

"Oh, that was well done, Jade Flower," the Old Old One said, patting the little girl on the shoulder. "Now if we had only the strong breezes of autumn we could also try the truth of our saying, 'It is easier to thread needles by moonlight than to hold a thread straight when the wind blows.'"

XXIII
THE LOST STAR PRINCESS

Aᴆᴛᴇʀ the needle contest everyone sat silent for a time,
looking up at the stars that twinkled in the sky above the
Garden of Sweet Smells. The eldest son of the old woman
was first to break the silence. He pointed with his fan to a
cluster of specially large stars and then touched Ah Shung
on the arm.

"How many bright stars do you see just there, Little
Bear?" he said to his son. The boy counted carefully.

"I see six," he replied.

"Six is correct," said his father, "but once there were

seven stars in that group. Our honored Lao Lao knows what has become of the seventh one which is now not among them. I have heard her tell the tale often, but I should greatly enjoy hearing her repeat it for you." The dignified man in his gown of softly rustling silk made a polite little bow toward his old mother. Even in cozy family meetings like this he was careful to keep all the rules of behavior for a good son.

"Yes, it is well that the young should know the wonders of ancient times, my son, and gladly will I tell them the story of the lost Star Princess," the old woman said, moving her round silken fan backward and forward.

"Thousands upon thousands of years gone by, my heart's jewels," she began, "there lived a good old man whose name was Sing Wu. No money had he, no house to live in, and only a few rags to cover his body. So poor was Sing Wu that he had to knock on the drums at the gates of the rich and beg his food from them. But we are fed from heaven, my children, and there was always someone with a generous heart to put rice into his bowl.

"Each night this poor beggar took shelter upon the steps of the great temple that stood on a hill, for he hoped that the good people who came there to pray would take pity upon him. And whenever a coin fell into his outstretched hand he would buy with it rice which he shared with other beggars more hungry than he.

"Now Yu Huang, the Jade Emperor of the Heavenly Kingdom, looked down on Sing Wu and not one of the poor man's acts of kindness escaped his all-seeing eye. One day Yu Huang decided that the time had come to reward so good a man, and he sent a heavenly messenger to summon Su Chee the youngest of his daughters, the seven Star Princesses.

" 'O daughter whom I love as I love my right hand,' the Jade Emperor said. 'I am about to send you on a journey. It will be long and it will be hard. You will have to leave your comfortable place here in the sky, but you will gain pleasure from a good deed well done and you will not be sorry.'

" 'Speak, Glorious One, speak! Your daughter only waits your shining words,' said the Star Princess, Su Chee.

" 'On the steps of the temple that stands on the hill in the City of Sweet Peace there dwells a beggar whose name is Sing Wu. He is old. He is poor. You will find him in rags. But in all the years of his life he has never done wrong.'

" 'When the night falls you must leave the heavens. You must go down on the earth and seek out Sing Wu. You will find him lost in a deep slumber which I have sent down upon him. Wake him. Give him youth. Give him riches. Dress him in silks and take him for your husband. And, best beloved of all my star daughters, if you do your duty well, at the end of twelve moons I shall send for you to return to your place in the heavens.'

"Swift as the lightning, Su Chee sped down to earth. Those who were awake on that night thought that all the stars were falling from the dome of the sky, for hundreds of star maidens accompanied Su Chee on the first stage of her journey. And the temple on the hill in the City of Sweet Peace was flooded with light.

"On the white stone temple steps Su Chee found the good beggar sound asleep. Gently she laid her hand on his shoulder and softly she spoke to him, 'Wake, Sing Wu, wake! Your bride awaits you. See, I am ready to eat our wedding rice and to drink our wedding cup.'

"Sing Wu rubbed his eyes. 'Who mocks poor Sing Wu?' he cried. 'What fair maiden is this that would marry a beggar with no home but these hard steps and no rice in his eating bowl? Where would a beggar find wine for a wedding?'

" 'Rise, Sing Wu,' said the Star Princess. 'All that is changed. Now you are young. Now you are rich. The Jade Emperor, Yu Huang, himself has sent you these gifts because you have been such a good man.'

"The beggar jumped to his feet. He thought he must be dreaming, for he found indeed that he felt as strong and as lively as when he was young. His rags had turned into silken garments as fine as those of the richest men in all the great city.

"And so they were married, my children, the good temple beggar and the lovely Star Princess. For nearly twelve moons Sing Wu and Su Chee dwelt together in happiness in a rich house with many courts and the finest of furnishings.

"But one afternoon, as the Star Princess gathered flowers in her garden, a powerful mandarin who lived in the neighboring household looked over the wall. He was so struck by her beauty that he could think of nothing else. He wrote poems about her skin which he said was more fair than the moonlight, about her black eyes that were shaped like the almond seed, and about her wee feet so like the lily buds.

"This wicked man vowed that if he could not have Su Chee for his wife he would pray the Jade Emperor to send so much rain from the sky that it would drown all the people in the City of Sweet Peace. He dared even to call upon Sing Wu himself and proposed to exchange his own wife for Su Chee. He offered to give Sing Wu so much money that it could never be counted. Sing Wu was angry, and he quickly ordered the wicked mandarin out of his courts.

"But when Su Chee heard of the mandarin's visit she was not angry at all. 'It would be far better for you to accept the mandarin's money,' she said to Sing Wu, who gaped at her in amazement. 'Wait, my husband, do not speak, and I will tell you how that may be. I am no earthly woman. I am a Star Princess, the daughter of the great Jade Emperor himself. I belong in the heavens with my sisters, the stars, and there I must return within just a few days. Yu Huang has sent for me.'

"'Go to the mandarin,' the Star Princess continued, 'agree to his plan and be not afraid. He shall not wed me even though I enter his gate as a bride.'

"Sing Wu was sad at the thought of losing his beloved Star Princess. But he thought to himself, 'If she is indeed the daughter of the Heavenly Emperor, I suppose it cannot be helped.' So he made all the arrangements and the last day of the twelfth moon of Su Chee's stay upon earth was chosen as the lucky time for her arrival at the mandarin's gate.

"Such preparations as the mandarin made for her coming! Musicians from five cities, the best cooks in the empire, and hundreds of guests all were assembled. The walls were hung with the finest embroideries and paintings, and the gardens were ablaze with flowers from all parts of the land.

"But when Su Chee's red sedan chair was set down inside the mandarin's gate, she hurried quickly to the inner court which had been made ready for her. The guests waited impatiently to see her, but no bride appeared. At last the mandarin sent a maid servant to knock on her door. 'The master is waiting. The guests grow impatient, Honored Lady,' she said. 'They beg you to shed the light of your presence upon them.'

" 'Tell your master,' Su Chee replied, 'that I am not well. Bid the guests enjoy themselves until evening. When supper is ready I surely will join them.'

"So the afternoon melted into the night and the court-yards were lighted with a thousand gay-colored lanterns. Dish after dish came from the kitchens, and the tables in the courtyard were spread with a feast fit for an emperor.

" 'Go to your master now,' Su Chee commanded her

maid servant. 'Tell him I am ready. Bid him gather his guests about the spread tables and have the musicians play their most glorious tunes.'

"The tongues of the guests were hushed with wonder when at last Su Chee appeared. Her red silken robe shone like the sunrise, and seven bright stars gleamed in the crown she wore on her head. But fear struck the hearts of the guests as they saw the stern look on the face of the Star Princess. Her eyes blazed like fire as she spoke to the mandarin thus: 'Wicked fool, not content with your own lovely wife, you have tried to steal away the wife of your neighbor. You have dared to raise your eyes to a Star Princess, the daughter of Yu Huang, the Ruler of the Heavenly Kingdom. My father is angry. He bids me punish your impudence.'

"And with this, the Star Princess brought her two little hands sharply together. With her first clap the wicked mandarin disappeared like a puff of smoke in the air. With her second, the houses and gardens and all the fine courtyards were gone, and in their place there stood a broad lake. The servants were turned into fishes, and the musicians and guests became frogs that croak in the night. People say that the frogs which make so much noise in their pools on summer evenings are really the mandarin's guests calling for their lost feast.

"Listen carefully, my children, to our own frogs in the Pool of the Goldfish. Can you hear them calling, 'Tea table, tea table, tea table'? Or do you think they are saying, 'Food's ready, food's ready, food's ready'?"

"What became of Su Chee, Lao Lao?" Yu Lang asked. "Did she go back to her place in the sky?"

"Yes, Jade Flower, Su Chee flew back again to the Heavenly Kingdom. But she did not take her old place in the midst of her sisters. 'You are changed by your visit on earth, my star daughter,' the Jade Emperor said to her when she arrived. 'Because you lived for so long with your earthly husband, Sing Wu, you will ever be interested in what goes on in the world of men. To reward you for doing your duty so well I shall give you a new place in the heavens. You shall shine more brightly than any one of your six sisters. And you shall shine, set apart, where all can admire you.'

"Do you see that star there below the six shining sisters?" Grandmother Ling asked, pointing out a bright star a little apart from the others. "That is the lost Star Princess, Su Chee. Every clear night she sends down her bright light on our fields. She makes the grain grow, and she still brings luck to those who are kind and good like Sing Wu."

XXIV

THE MANDARIN
AND THE BUTTERFLIES

ONE warm summer afternoon Yu Lang and the other girls of the household sat with the Old Old One in the summer house at the very end of the garden. Each had a needle threaded with bright silk in one hand and a bit of cloth in the other. The Old Old One herself was making the scales on the back of a twisting green dragon. Some

198

of the girls were embroidering rose and blue flowers on heavy silk which would later be used for the sides of their own tiny shoes. Yu Lang was setting small stitches in the pattern of a gay butterfly.

"A butterfly for joy!" the Old Old One exclaimed as she examined the little girl's work. "A wise man of ancient days once had a dream in which he thought he was changed into a butterfly. He drifted pleasantly from one flower to another, and from each he sipped the sirup hidden deep in its heart. When he awoke he fancied that he could still see the beautiful blossoms, that he could still smell their perfume, and that he could still taste their sweet honey. Never had he known such happiness, and so he adopted the butterfly as his symbol for pleasure and joy. And such, my maids of the needle, it has been ever since."

"See what I have caught, Lao Lao," Ah Shung cried just then, running to the summer house from the garden path where he had been playing. The boy held a long bamboo rod in his hand. One end of it had been slit, and a small bamboo crosspiece had been used to wedge its ends apart. In a bush in a far corner he had found some thick cobwebs, and he had twisted the split end of his stick around and around in the sticky mass.

With this homemade trap Ah Shung had been chasing the butterflies that flittered hither and thither in the Garden of Sweet Smells. He had only to touch them and the pretty creatures were held fast in the sticky cobweb on the end of his rod.

The butterfly which Ah Shung brought to show the Old Old One had bright-colored wings of blue, green, and yellow. Holding it carefully between his thumb and forefinger, the boy laid it down beside the butterfly pattern which Yu Lang was working with her embroidery silks.

"Mine is the prettiest," he said.

"But mine will last longer," his sister replied.

"Yu Lang may be sure that her butterfly will bring her only joy," Grandmother Ling said, smiling. "But you, Little Bear, must take care how you handle the live butterflies. If you do not treat them gently they may bring trouble upon you as they did upon Mandarin Wang. Stop your chase for a moment, O Mighty Hunter, and I will tell you how the butterflies evened their score with that cruel man.

"This mandarin, Wang, held a place of importance in a great city. He had received an appointment as judge before whom wrongdoers were brought to be sentenced. He alone could decide how much money in fines they should pay into the treasury or how long they should sit on the crowded streets wearing the 'wooden necktie.' "

Grandmother Ling was speaking of the wooden board of punishment which was locked round the neck of prisoners in old China. It was very uncomfortable for it was so broad that the unlucky person who wore it could not get his hands to his face to brush mosquitoes away or to put food into his mouth.

"Inside Wang's gate," the old woman continued, "there

were many fine courtyards and the mandarin's money boxes were always full to the top. No other mandarin had finer food nor better rice wine than Wang. And none paid more attention to his own comfort and amusement.

"One summer Mandarin Wang thought of a new way of giving himself pleasure. When a wrongdoer was brought before him, he would not fine him, nor would he put round his neck the 'wooden necktie.' Instead he would say, 'Worthless fellow, you shall go free, and you shall pay no fine for your offense, if you will only bring me tomorrow one hundred live butterflies.' The prisoner would be astonished, of course, but he would rejoice at getting off so easily. And the next day he would appear at the mandarin's gate, the hundred butterflies safely caged in a basket of woven bamboo.

"Dressed in his official robes, with his judge's hat still on his head, as though he were going to pay an important visit, Wang would take his place on the shady veranda. There would be sweet cakes to eat and rice wine to drink, close at his hand. Then he would call together all the women and the girls who lived within his walls, and he would command them to play before him the Game of the Butterflies. With hairs pulled from their own heads, the women would tie tiny weights made of twisted paper to each butterfly's body so that it could not fly far away. Then they would set it free.

"In the sunshine the butterflies flitted slowly about the mandarin's courtyard like scraps of bright silks blown by

*The women and girls chased the butterflies with their fans
to make them fly faster*

a wind. The women and girls chased them with their fans to make them fly faster. It was a gay sight, the hundred butterflies with their hundred gay colors, and the girls and the women in their summer gowns of soft flowerlike hues.

"One afternoon, when the Game of the Butterflies had just ended, and the maids had gone back to their inner courtyards, Mandarin Wang sat and dozed upon his veranda. His rice wine had made him so drowsy that his chin at last dropped upon his silken breast and he slept soundly.

"During his slumber his soul made a voyage into the land of dreams, where he saw a fair maiden dressed in colors as gay as a butterfly's wing. He was about to pay her polite compliments when she spoke to him sternly. 'O Cruel Wang, I have come to warn you,' she said. 'I am a Butterfly Princess. Your selfish Game of the Butterflies has brought suffering and sorrow to my poor sisters. Some even have died. And for this you shall pay.'

"Before Mandarin Wang could utter a word in reply, the maiden had changed herself into a huge butterfly and had flown out of sight. Then the mandarin felt the touch of a hand on his shoulder.

" 'Wake, master, wake!' a servant was calling. 'The governor comes! The governor comes! He is even now at the gate.'

"Wang jumped to his feet. He hurriedly straightened the folds of his gown, and he hastened through the courts to meet the great man. Breathless, he made his bows of politeness as the visitor dismounted from his sedan chair. The mandarin knew well that the governor would be angry if all was not done according to custom and if he did not receive the full honor due him.

"To Wang's surprise his guest did not return his bows or his greeting. Instead his face flamed with anger. 'How dare vou receive me thus, O Man of Little Respect?' the governor cried.

" 'Excellent One of Surpassing Goodness,' Wang said, bowing again and again, 'how am I lacking in respect to your importance? Have I not kept the custom and met you here at the gate? Have I not bowed low before you as I would bow to my grandfather? How can I have offended you?'

" 'Is it the custom, is it being respectful, to greet a guest like myself in the costume of a traveling player?' the governor asked, eying poor Wang with great disapproval. 'Look at your hat, your official hat, with flowers upon it! Are you a woman that you should deck yourself so? What could be more unseemly?'"

"The mandarin looked dazed. His knees knocked together as he took off his precious hat with the judge's button upon it. To his surprise he saw that a garland of white flowers had been twisted about it. He stammered and stuttered as he tried to explain that he knew nothing about them. The governor would not believe him and declared he would take Wang's position away from him if such a thing ever should happen again.

"Wang bowed his head meekly. His brain was still whirling, and it was only when the governor had departed that he could gather his wits together. It was then he remembered the threat of the Butterfly Princess. At once he knew that it was she who had put the flowers round his hat and that this was her way of punishing him for his cruel Game of the Butterflies. He also knew he would never dare to play it again."

XXV

HENG O, THE MOON LADY

For DAYS, in every court inside the bright red gate of the Lings, there had been comings and goings quite out of the ordinary. In the Garden of Sweet Smells blue-clad workmen were planting in pots new flowers just coming into bloom. The maid servants were putting the houses in order under the watchful eyes of their mistresses. Treasures that had not been taken out of the chests since this time last year were being arranged on tables in the reception halls, where guests might inspect them.

The kitchen was perhaps the busiest of all the little low buildings that stood round the courtyards. There the men cooks and the younger women of the Ling family were working from morning till night, making little round cakes stuffed with almonds and orange peel, melon seeds and sugar, and other good things. They were decorating these cakes with tiny rabbits and toads and pagodas made of sugar. Besides, they were preparing other delicious dishes which they always ate in their celebration of the Moon Lady's birthday on the Fifteenth Day of the Eighth Moon.

The Old Mistress herself, with Fu, the number one servant, and her maid, Huang Ying, spent the days going from one court to the other, directing the work of preparing for the feast that was about to take place. Ah Shung and Yu Lang followed her like a shadow. They could hardly wait for the Moon Lady's birthday party to begin. Each time they saw packages brought in through the bright red gate they whispered to each other, "Perhaps it is a pagoda or a moon rabbit for us." Their old nurse, Wang Lai, had taken them to the fair in the temple grounds, where they had seen the toysellers with their trays of painted clay rabbits and gay-colored toy pagodas.

The Moon Lady's birthday table was set out in the open Courtyard of Politeness. It was covered with a red cloth and laid with five plates filled with fruits as round as the

round moon itself. There were apples and peaches, pome-
granates and grapes. A pyramid of the little moon-cakes
rose high into the air. Candles in pairs and urns filled with
incense-sticks stood here and there.

The children were charmed with the splendid clay pagoda which stood in the center to represent the palace of
the Moon Lady. Inside it a burning candle sent light shining through each tiny paper windowpane, just as lights
shone from the houses round the courtyard. But the boys
and girls were even more interested in the tall clay Moon
Rabbit in his mandarin's gown, standing up on his long
hind legs just like a man. Ah Shung had made a little
bundle of bean stalks, the Moon Rabbit's favorite food,
and Yu Lang had been allowed to place it herself at the
feet of the statue. Near the birthday table, on the courtyard wall, there was a bright printed poster that showed
the Moon Rabbit under his cinnamon tree, pounding the
pill-of-long-life in his little bowl.

"Heng O, the Moon Lady, comes at last," the Old Old
One said to her family as they stood together out in the
courtyard. "How she lights up the sky! The moon is
larger tonight than at any time of the year."

Everyone watched the round silver disk come slowly out
from its hiding place behind the big willow tree. The children gazed at it in wonder. They thought they could
trace the outline of the Moon Rabbit upon its bright face,
and sometimes they thought they could also find a toad
or the Moon Lady, Heng O, herself. Tonight Yu Lang

imagined that she could see an open door in the moon, for she had been taught to believe that each year on her birthday the Moon Lady left her shining palace and came down to earth.

The Old Old One led the procession to the birthday table which they had spread in honor of the Moon Lady. She knelt on the stones of the courtyard before it and swayed back and forth in a respectful kowtow. At the same time she said this little prayer to the Queen of the Night:

> *"O Light One,*
> *O Bright One,*
> *O Wheel of Ice,*
> *O Mirror Bright*
> *We bow tonight,*
> *Bless thou our rice!"*

Ah Shung's older sister played sweet tunes on her four-stringed lute while the Ling family waited, to allow time for the Moon Lady and the Moon Rabbit to partake of the good things which they had spread out for them. When the feasting was over, they sat for a time out in the moonlight. It was the end of summer and in the fields beyond the city the yellow grain was being cut. But the air was still warm, and sweet smells were wafted across the courtyards by the soft night breeze.

"Tonight I must tell you how the lovely Heng O flew up to the Moon, and how the Moon Rabbit came to be," the Old Old One said as she gathered her grandchildren about her. "It was long, long ago in the time when the Emperors of China came from the family of Shia. One day as the Son of Heaven rode forth from the palace in his yellow sedan chair he saw upon the highway a man with long arrows and a huge red bow in his hands. The Emperor had never seen another bow like it, and he stopped to examine it.

" 'I am Hou Ye, the bowman,' the man replied to his questions. 'With my red bow I shoot arrows from one side of the world to the other. And swift as their flight, I ride on the winds. I am lighter than air because I eat only flowers.' The Emperor was astonished. He hardly believed these words of Hou Ye.

" 'Do you see yonder pine tree on the top of that mountain, O Bowman?' he asked, pointing to a high peak that rose clear and sharp against the blue sky. 'If you can indeed shoot from one side of the world to the other, send an arrow through its branches. If you can do that, we shall give you the post of Imperial Archer.'

"The bowman took aim. He bent his red bow, and, straight as a bird flies, his arrow sped to the pine tree on the top of the far mountain. At once the bowman jumped upon a passing wind and flew off to fetch it back to the chair of the Son of Heaven.

"The Emperor kept his promise. He made Hou Ye Imperial Archer, and again and again he called upon him to aim his red bow at some enemy. When a wicked serpent or a tiger did harm to a village, Hou Ye was sent forth to kill him. When the Heavenly Dog tried to eat up the moon, Hou Ye shot an arrow into the sky to drive him away. When the rains did not fall, he would shoot his sharp arrows into the clouds to remind the sky dragons that water was needed.

"One year there came a terrible flood. The rivers spilled out over the fields. People were drowned. Houses and animals were carried away. Sadness filled the land. The Emperor ordered Hou Ye to take his magic bow and seek out Ho Po, the great God of the Waters, who was causing the flood. Quickly the archer mounted the wind and he soon found the water spirit. He shot his swift arrows and he wounded Ho Po so that he flew far away and never returned to do evil again. Immediately the waters flowed back into the rivers. The country was saved.

"Now, my children, the water spirit had a beautiful sister whose name was Heng O. Hou Ye saw her standing beside her brother, Ho Po, but she was so fair to look upon that he could not bring himself to wound her. When he bent his red bow he was careful to aim his arrow at her thick raven-black hair which she wore in a coil high on her head. The water spirit's sister was so grateful to him for saving her life that she gladly consented to become his wife.

"Not long after, a dreadful thing happened. In the sky there appeared not one sun but ten. Ten round burning disks sent their fierce rays down on the earth. Leaves died on their branches. Grass blades burned to a crisp. No grain could grow. In the terrible heat the water dried up in the wells and the streams. Quickly the Emperor called for Hou Ye.

" 'O Archer,' he said, 'save us as you have saved us before! The soothsayers declare that in each of those suns there lives a golden raven upon whose life the sun's heat and light depends. Take your red bow and shoot the gold ravens! Shoot quickly, O Archer, or we shall all die.'

"Hou Ye drew back his bow. He turned it up toward the sky. Zing-ng-ng! went his arrow as it flew straight and sure to the first of the blazing suns. And before you could finish that moon-cake in your hand, Ah Shung, that sun was gone out of the sky. Zing-ng-ng! A second arrow sped upward to find the second sun. And that ball of fire also was gone. Three, four, five, six, seven, eight, nine sun ravens were killed by the arrows of Hou Ye.

"The archer was just taking aim at the tenth when a voice came from the clouds. 'Hold, Archer,' it said, 'listen to the Sun God. Leave one sun in the sky so that the earth may be lighted. Without its brightness and warmth no one could live. Take care how you shoot!' So Hou Ye stayed his hand and the tenth sun still shines, high up there in the heavens.

"The fame of this deed spread far and wide over the earth. It reached the palace of the Empress of the West on the Kun Lun Mountains, and she sent a swift whirlwind to bring Hou Ye before her. With her own hand she put into his a precious pill-of-long-life.

" 'When you swallow this, Mighty Archer,' she said, 'you shall be carried to the heavens, where you will live forever. But do not swallow it now. The time is not ready. For twelve months you must prepare yourself. Hide the pill away. Keep it a secret until the hour comes for you to fly away to the sky.'

"When Hou Ye returned home he followed the advice of the Lady of Kun Lun. He hid the pill-of-long-life carefully up under the roof, and he said never a word about it to anyone, not even to his dear wife, the lovely Heng O.

"It was not long after that the Emperor sent his Imperial Archer on a journey to the south, to fight with a strange man who had round popping eyes and a single sharp tooth from which he got his name, 'Chisel Tooth.'

"While her husband was away Heng O found the time long. One day, as she was going here and there through the house, she saw a bright light high up under the roof. Sweet perfume filled the air. She easily found that the light and the perfume came from the pearly white pill-of-long-life which Hou Ye had hidden. She put the pill into her mouth and, as soon as she had swallowed it, she felt light as a kite and she found she could fly like a bird.

"When her husband returned from killing old Chisel Tooth, he discovered that his precious pill-of-long-life had disappeared, and he sought out Heng O to ask what had become of it. In fear of his anger, she flew out of the window and up to the sky, where she hid in the moon. Hardly had she landed than a fit of coughing seized her, and out of her mouth flew the shell of the pill, which straightway became a rabbit of purest white jade. You can see the Jade Rabbit now on the shining moon disk there above us. Some say Heng O was punished for stealing the pill-of-long-life. They declare she was turned into a toad. But I like to think she is still a fair lady.

"You can imagine that at first Hou Ye was cross," the Old Old One continued. "He mounted a swift wind and rode this way and that way, seeking his wife. The Empress of Kun Lun took pity upon him when he sought her aid. 'Do not fret, Archer,' she said. 'You shall dwell in the sun and you, too, shall live forever.' And she gave him a magic cake to eat, in order that he should be able to withstand the fierce heat in his new palace.

"Yet another gift Hou Ye received from the Empress of Kun Lun, a golden bird with a red comb standing high on his head. 'You have been told how to make the sun rise,' said the Empress, 'but how should you know when the hour has come? This golden bird with the red comb will wake you each morning.' And that golden bird which Hou Ye took with him to his palace must have been the ancestor of the roosters in our stable yard that wake us from our sleep each day when the skies first see the sun.

"In his sun palace Hou Ye felt more kindly toward his wife, Heng O. With a charm which the Western Empress had given him, he made his way to the moon to tell her he had forgiven her. He found the moon a sad empty place, ice cold, and with no plants but the cinnamon tree under which the Jade Rabbit stood mixing the pill-of-long-life in his little stone bowl.

"Hou Ye built for his wife her beautiful palace in the moon, and he arranged to visit her there. It is when he comes to see her on the night of the fifteenth of every month that she is largest and fullest. When he goes away she grows paler and paler, and she does not grow bright again until it is time for his visit once more."

"Does Heng O truly come down to earth tonight, Lao Lao?" Yu Lang asked when the old woman ended her story of the Moon Lady.

"I have heard that she does, Precious Pearl," said Grandmother Ling. "They say she goes everywhere and that she listens to the wishes of those who do her honor. But take care, little Yu Lang! If you utter a wish, be sure to speak clearly. There is a story about an old woman who lived long, long ago and who once saw the Moon Lady. When the Queen of the Night appeared before her, the old woman was so dazzled by her bright beauty that she could not speak a word. Heng O asked what she wished, but the woman was silent. At last she pulled herself together enough to move her trembling hand up and down over the lower part of her face. By so doing she meant to show the Moon Lady that she wished only for rice to put into her mouth.

" 'Well, it seems very strange, but if that is what you want you shall have it,' the Moon Lady promised. You see, Heng O had quite misunderstood the old woman's meaning. This was clear the next morning, for there was no more rice than before in the old woman's eating bowl. But when she raised her hand to her mouth she found to her dismay that the Moon Lady had covered her face with gray whiskers. And she had to wait for a year, until Heng O's next birthday, before she could wish her beard off again."

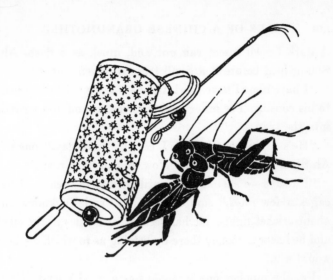

XXVI
CHENG'S FIGHTING CRICKET

ONE AUTUMN DAY, as soon as they had finished their lessons with Scholar Shih in the Court of Learning, Ah Shung and his cousins hurried along the paths of the Garden of Sweet Smells. The boys ran on tiptoe, and no one said a word lest he should frighten the little brown crickets for which they meant to hunt.

"Hark! Over there!" Ah Shung whispered as a faint chirping was heard upon the little rock mountain in the midst of the garden. The boy poked with a twig among the stones that had been laid up to make the tiny hill.

A dark brown insect ran out and, quick as a flash, Ah Shung held before it a small trap of woven bamboo.

"I have him! I have him! And he is a big one," he called to his cousins. The other boys gathered round and peered into the trap.

"He's as big as the one I caught yesterday," one of Ah Shung's cousins cried. "Now we can fight them."

"Fu says we should wait until they have been in their cages a few days," said Ah Shung, "and Fu knows all about cricket fights. He has seen great battles in the city and he has won money there by betting as to which cricket would win."

Fu, the number one servant, was a good friend of all the children inside the red gate of the Lings. He had himself made the bamboo cricket traps for the boys and had told them where to look for the special kind of crickets that fight. He even got them some grains of rice and bits of green lettuce to feed their tiny prisoners.

There was excitement among the children and amusement among the grownups as the boys made their plans for their cricket fight. Their fathers showed them how to tie stiff hairs to the ends of small bamboo sticks. They explained how these were used to tickle the wee warriors until they were angry enough to strike out. Wang Lai, the nurse, brought the boys a round wooden bowl upon whose rough bottom the crickets' feet would not slip and slide.

The Old Old One had the place of honor at the stone

table in the garden, upon which the fighting bowl was set down. Since the autumn day was cool, she was wearing a jacket lined with light fur, and the children were warm in suits well padded with cotton.

All the members of the family gathered to watch the great fight. Even the men laid aside their books and their writing brushes and left their library on the Courtyard of Politeness to give advice to their small sons as to how best to manage their crickets.

Ah Shung and his cousin opened the door of their cricket traps and shook their tiny fighters gently out into the bowl. Each brown cricket was only about an inch long. At first they stood still, as if they did not know what to do. Then the boys tickled their feelers with the stiff hairs on the ends of their bamboo sticks. The crickets grew cross. They rubbed their front wings together, making angry chirping noises. Then they dashed into the fight. They rushed at each other. They locked their tusks together. Over and over they rolled on the bottom of the wooden bowl while the spectators cheered.

What a shout there was when Ah Shung's cricket pushed the other brown fighter over upon his back so that he could not get up! The boy clapped his hands and cried, "Mine wins! Mine wins!"

"But my cricket is not through yet," Ah Shung's cousin declared. "Give him time to rest and he will yet beat."

"It is not for nothing that we say men are 'as brave as a cricket,'" said Grandmother Ling. "A cricket will fight so long as he has breath. So while we wait for these two to rest up for their next battle I will tell you a story about the marvelous cricket which brought fame and fortune to a poor man named Cheng who lived in a small village.

"This all took place long ago, when cricket fighting was even more loved by men than it is today. The Emperor who then sat upon the Dragon Throne so enjoyed seeing battles between these fighting insects that he demanded, as taxes, crickets instead of money or rice.

"One year the governor of a certain district sent as a present to the Son of Heaven a splendid fighting cricket. So bravely did it battle against all its enemies that the Emperor was delighted, and he commanded this governor to send him each autumn many others just like it.

"Now the governor could not fulfill the Emperor's order himself and so, in his turn, he commanded the head of each little village to get crickets for him. In one of these villages the headman was this Cheng. He was a poor man who had tried many times to pass the examinations for a better office, but who always had failed. When he received the governor's order for a fine fighting cricket he wrung his hands sadly. 'I might as well throw myself in the river!' he cried to his wife. 'The rich men from the city pay such high prices for crickets that it would take all we have inside our gate to buy even one from the cricket hunters.'

" 'Then you had best go out and catch one yourself,'

Cheng's wife replied. Poor Cheng took a bamboo tube and a little trap like Ah Shung's and went out to the grave mounds, where the crickets were most likely to be. He poked about under the stones. He looked under the bushes. He peered into every hole he saw in the ground. But when he returned to his home the three puny creatures inside his bamboo tube were so weak that when the governor saw them he ordered poor Cheng to be given one hundred blows of the bamboo rod. And he commanded him to bring a really good fighting cricket before the moon ended.

"Poor Cheng's back was so sore that he could not spend long hours searching for a cricket. His wife thought and thought as to how she could help him. At last she gathered together a few pennies and went to seek out the new fortune teller who had lately come to the village. When she returned to her home she bore in her hand a piece of white paper upon which there was drawn the picture of a hill behind the temple. At the foot of this hill there were shown a heap of stones and a hopping toad.

" 'Ai-yah, my husband,' she wailed, 'I have thrown our money away. The only thing I got in return for it is this silly picture which the fortune teller made with his hair pen.'

" 'Not so silly as you think,' said Chang when he saw the paper. 'No doubt this is telling me where to find a fine cricket. That temple is the very one to the east of our village. I shall go there at once.'

"Cheng left his bed and hobbled to the hill behind the

old temple. Beside the pile of stones, which the drawing had shown, he took his seat, and he watched and he watched for the cricket to appear. 'Ai, I might as well look for a mustard seed,' he said to himself, for no little brown insect could he find among the stones.

"But just then out of the bushes there came a fat toad. Chang rose from his seat and followed the creature as it hopped under a bush. When the man drew back the branches he saw on the ground a cricket so splendid that his heart jumped for joy. After a little trouble he captured it and put it gently inside his tube of bamboo.

"How the Cheng family nursed that cricket! They fed it on chestnuts and meat. They brought it water clear as a crystal from a faraway spring. And they tended it carefully against the time when the governor should send a messenger for it.

"But Cheng had a small son, about the age of Ah Shung. And one day, my children, when his mother was away washing clothes in the stream, the naughty boy uncovered the bowl in which the precious cricket was kept. With a mighty spring the insect leaped out of his prison. The boy ran after it, but, try as he would, he could not catch it, and the insect escaped.

"When Cheng came home that evening he flew into a fury when he heard the cricket was gone. He called for his son, but no trace of the child could be found. They searched and they searched, and at last they discovered his body at the bottom of a deep well. They thought at first he was drowned. Later they saw he still breathed, although they could not rouse him out of his slumber.

"The father thought more about his lost cricket than his sleeping boy. All through the night he sat gazing at the empty bowl. The sun was lighting the sky when suddenly he heard the faint chirp of a cricket just outside the house door. Cheng first thought the insect might be his own splendid lost cricket, but he soon saw it was a smaller one, of a poor reddish-brown color. He was about to let the cricket go when it suddenly hopped up on his sleeve. 'After all, it is a handsome little fellow,' he said, and he decided to keep it.

" 'I will just try it out, even though it is small,' he thought, and so he arranged for a fight with a neighbor whose crickets were noted for winning in the village cricket fights. That neighbor laughed when he saw Cheng's small red-brown insect. He showed him how much bigger and stronger his dark-brown fighters looked, and he scoffed so loudly that poor Cheng was ready to give up the fight.

" 'But we may as well have some amusement,' Cheng said. 'Let us fight just the same, and if my cricket is wounded it will be no great matter.'

"So they put the two crickets into a fighting bowl. Cheng's cricket lay quite still. It was not until it had been tickled and tickled with the pig's hair that it even moved. Oh, but then you should have seen that little red-brown cricket! It gave one mighty leap and attacked the other cricket so bravely and fiercely that the larger cricket would have been killed if the fight had not been stopped. The little red-brown cricket stood up on its hind legs and chirped with joy at its splendid victory.

"Cheng was about to pick his cricket up when a rooster walked over toward the bowl. It started to snap the cricket up in its beak when the tiny fighter leaped on his comb and held on tight with its tusks while the rooster squawked with pain. Joy filled the heart of Cheng and he put his cricket away in a cage of bamboo and took it to the governor. That important person was not at all pleased at the sight of such a small red-brown insect, and when Cheng told him of the bravery of his little fighter, he would not believe him. Not until it had beaten all the fighting crickets in the governor's palace was he convinced that this cricket of Cheng's was fit to send to the Emperor.

"The governor put Cheng's cricket in a cage made of ivory and jade, and he took it himself to the Dragon Throne. Never had there been seen such a fighter at the Emperor's court. A cricket that could beat enemies three times his size! A wee insect that could get the best of a rooster! It was found that Cheng's cricket even would dance when music was played. So of course it had a place of honor in the Emperor's palace.

"In return for his gift, the governor received from the Emperor magnificent presents of horses and silks, and in his turn he rewarded Cheng, from whom the marvelous cricket had come. He persuaded the judge to pass Cheng in his next examinations, and he gave him a much better position than that of headman of the village.

"Best of all, in a short time Cheng's son, who had been sleeping for many a day, opened his eyes.

" 'Where am I?' were the first words the boy spoke. 'I must have been dreaming. I thought the gods turned me into a cricket and that I fought a great fight here in our village. It seemed to me that I even conquered a rooster. Then I went to a far place where I fought other crickets and where I lived in a cage of ivory and jade.'

"The boy's father knew then that the Emperor of Heaven had sent his son's spirit into the little red-brown cricket in order to save him from death. Cheng did not forget to give thanks for the return of his son's soul, nor for the good luck that each passing year brought. In a short time he grew rich. He had houses and fields, and he became the most important person in his neighborhood. And all because of a little red-brown cricket even smaller than these in our fighting bowl."

XXVII

THE MAID IN THE MIRROR

I SHALL NEVER LEARN to make word pictures so well as you, Lao Lao," Ah Shung sighed as he watched his grandmother's hand moving over the strip of thin white rice-straw paper which lay on the table before her.

"Ah yes, Small Bear, you will perhaps write even better if you work well with Scholar Shih in the Court of Learning," the old woman replied. "And Yu Lang also must soon begin to learn how to hold the hair pen. Even though she is a girl, I intend that she shall be taught to

read and to write, just as I was. Others may be satisfied
with teaching their girl children to keep house, to embroider, and to play on the lute. But a dull needle will
not go through cloth half so swiftly as a bright one, and
Yu Lang, as well as her brothers, needs to sharpen her
wits."

The Old Old One was noted for her skill with the Four
Gems of the Library, as she called her paper and her
rabbit-hair brush, her ink stone of carved gray stone with
its little well filled with water, and her sweet-smelling ink
stick of dried lampblack and pine oil. She knew how to dip
her ink stick in the water just long enough for it to make
a smooth black paste when she rubbed it on the little ink-
slab. Years of practicing with the brush had given her
great skill in making the delicate strokes of the word
pictures which the Chinese use in their writing.

"You should have seen my father use the hair pen," Lao
Lao said to the children who stood beside her table watching her make one stroke upward, another downward, a
third straight across. "He could copy the writing of the
best scholars in the empire so neatly that you could not
tell one from the other. To keep his brush-hand firm and
limber when he was not writing, he often held in it two
walnuts which he kept moving around and around. I can
remember their clicking noise now, as they rubbed against
one another. Sometimes my father allowed me to feel their
smooth polished shells which so much rubbing had turned
to the color of golden mahogany."

Grandmother Ling herself enjoyed copying the finely made word pictures in the old books in her study. She copied also the paintings on silk which were rolled up in her treasure chests. Often she made paintings out of her own mind, a rock or a mountain, a graceful stalk of bamboo or a spray of plum blossoms.

"You have not been doing well lately, Schoolmaster Shih tells me, Ah Shung," the Old Old One said as she dipped her brush in the fragrant ink paste. "You must work better. Remember, none holds so high a place as the scholar. The wealthiest man in the empire is not so important as one who has great learning. Also learning brings riches. If you study hard enough to pass the Emperor's examinations when you are older, high position and wealth will always be yours. So it was with young Lu. But, of course, he had to help him the lovely maid in the mirror."

The boy and the girl both pricked up their ears at the mention of a maid in a mirror. That sounded as though there might be a story near the door of the Old Old One's memory. But they did not dare to ask for it so long as their grandmother's hand was moving over the paper. They knew one false motion might spoil her whole page. But they breathed sighs of relief when she laid down her brush and sat back in her chair.

"You would like to hear that story?" Lao Lao asked, smiling at their shining eyes. "Well, my fingers are cramped. The brush no longer moves surely. I will tell the tale to you, and perhaps Ah Shung will remember it when things do not go well for him in our Courtyard of Learning.

"Lu was a young man who lived in days long gone by. His family were not rich, but they had determined that their son should be given as much schooling as any other youth in their city. They saved every penny in order that he might have the best teachers, and they watched each step he took along the road to the cells where the Emperor's examinations were held.

"Now, Lu was young and Lu sometimes was lazy. And there came a time when he did not work very hard over his books and his brushes. No matter how earnestly his father explained that once the examinations were passed he would be given a high position, Lu was not interested. He let his books lie closed and he spent his whole time in games with his friends or walking with his bird under the trees along the bank of the river.

"One summer day, as this idle young man strolled there with his bird cage in his hand, he met a maiden who said her name was Feng Hsien. She was of such shining beauty that both the sun and the moon seemed dim beside her. Feng Hsien smiled shyly at Lu. They exchanged words of greeting. And straightway the young man knew that he would have her for his wife or he would never be wed.

"Again and again Feng Hsien and Lu met on the river bank, and sweet were the hours they spent talking together. But one day, when it was time for them to part, the maiden grew sorrowful. 'Our meetings must end,' she said to the youth. 'You are wasting your days. You do not open a book. You do not lift the hair pen. The paste is dry on your ink stone. I shall not come again until you have passed your examinations. But I have brought you a present by means of which you sometimes may see me.' And she handed Lu a shining mirror just like that one that hangs over my bed."

The old woman pointed to a round disk of thin white metal which was hung up on the wall by its flat handle. There was so little glass in those days that most of the Chinese mirrors were made of polished metal instead. Lao Lao believed that this mirror helped to keep her safe from bad spirits. Often she had explained to the children that the spirits cannot bear to see their own faces. At the first glimpse of the silvery surface of the mirror they fly away in great haste. It is because of this that Lung-Er, the youngest Ling grandchild, always had a tiny glass mirror sewed upon his red cap. One could never tell when one might meet a bad spirit and it was well to take every care to drive it away. All these things flashed through Lao Lao's mind, and she paused for a moment. Then she went on with her story again.

"When she put the round mirror into his hand Feng Hsien said, 'My Honorable Friend, you will see my poor self in the face of this mirror. But you will see it there only when you have done well with your books and your writing brush.' And with that she was gone.

"Lu sadly turned his steps toward home. When he had

shut himself in the room which his family had given him for his study, he examined the mirror. He looked first at its back with the graceful bamboo leaves carved deep in its metal. Then he turned it around and peered at its smooth, polished, silvery face. There indeed he could see the figure of the lovely Feng Hsien. But the maid's back was turned, and she seemed to be moving away from him.

" 'Only when you have done well will you see me.' Lu repeated to himself the words Feng Hsien had said to him, and he sat down at his table and opened his books. His parents were overjoyed at the change in their son. From dawn until dark he worked in his study. He would not receive visitors. He no longer went forth to play games with his friends. His teachers had nothing but good to report of him. And each morning and each evening when Lu looked in the mirror he saw there the smiling face of Feng Hsien.

"But summer does not last forever, my children. And in climbing a hill the last step must be as firm as the first. In time Lu became weary of his well-doing. He began to go about once more with his friends. His books were seldom opened. His teachers shook their gray heads.

"Then one day the young man looked in the mirror and saw the fair maid with tears on her cheeks. She turned her back and began to move away as she had done on the day when Lu had first found her in the mirror. A wave of regret swept over the youth. He felt greatly ashamed, and he hurried to open his books. Once more he worked from dawn until dark. He hung the mirror where he could not fail to see when Feng Hsien was pleased and when she was sorrowful. His love for her grew so great and he worked so well that in just a few years he was ready to take the Emperor's examinations.

"Three times he went in and out of the little cells where the tests were given. Three times he passed and three times he returned in triumph to the house of his parents.

"What excitement there was in Lu's neighborhood when the red official notice of his final success was pasted upon his gate! Firecrackers were set off. Candles and incense burned in the Hall of the Ancestors so that they might know of the good fortune that had come to the family. Flags flew, and friends streamed in through the gate to congratulate the young man. Lu, dressed in a splendid new gown, rode about in a sedan chair to visit his friends, and there was a fine feast and a procession in honor of the occasion. In those early days women strewed flowers along the way, musicians played, and red banners tied upon leafy bamboo poles were carried before the young scholars.

"While the family celebration was still going on there came a knock at the gate of Lu's house, and there was announced a go-between who had been sent by the wealthiest man in the whole city to discuss the matter of a marriage between Lu and his daughter. Such is the power of learning, Ah Shung, that this man wished to bestow his fairest child, and many rich gifts with her, upon the son of this modest household.

"The young man's parents were overcome with joy at such good fortune. But, to their surprise, Lu himself would not listen to the go-between's words. 'I do not care how fair the young maiden may be, I will not wed her,' he said to his father. And he went into his study and closed the door tight.

"There he turned to the mirror to seek his beloved Feng Hsien. He found the maid's face wreathed in smiles, and as he looked it seemed to him that she stepped down out of the mirror and stood close beside him. 'Go back to the go-between, O Youth of Goodness and Wisdom,' the mirror maid said. 'Consent to the marriage he offers. Do not ask my reason, for I may not tell it. But believe me, all will be just as you most desire.'

"Before Lu could ask her one question the maiden had vanished. Try as he would he could not find even her shadow on the silvery face of the mirror. There was nothing for him to do but to follow her wishes, and, to his parents' great joy, the marriage was arranged.

"Lu's heart was sad, for he could not yet understand why his beloved Feng Hsien should wish him to marry another. And it was with downcast eyes that he met the bridal chair at the gate. However, his sorrow was soon turned to joy, my small ones. For when the bride stood before him, he found that, instead of a stranger, it was Feng Hsien herself.

"Never again did Lu see her face in the mirror. And never would she tell him what fairy had sent her spirit to meet him there on the river bank. As a matter of fact, he had no need to know that, and he had no need to look for her again in the mirror since all through his life she stood by his side.

"High position and riches and a beautiful bride! All these came to Lu because he paid attention to his books and his brush. And such good luck may come also to you, Little Bear, if you work hard with Scholar Shih in our Court of Learning."

XXVIII

MISS LIN, THE SEA GODDESS

Wʜᴀᴛ ɪs ᴛʜɪs, Lao Lao?" Ah Shung asked as he lifted a small object from the open drawer of the red lacquer cabinet that had been set on a table near the window of the Old Old One's room. The boy and his sister were sitting beside their grandmother, who was comfortably settled in her favorite chair of shining carved wood. Before them the two doors of the red cabinet were flung apart and one of its drawers, filled with trinkets and treasures, stood open under their eyes.

On the table were laid out several pieces of jewelry— bracelets and earrings of deep green jade stone, which the

Chinese prize more highly than the most glittering diamonds; rings of soft yellow gold with carvings upon them; and a dagger-shaped hairpin of silver with bits of red coral and sky-blue kingfisher feathers set in its pattern.

There were some pointed silver fingernail shields, three inches long. These had belonged to the children's grandfather, who had allowed the nails on his left hand to grow until they were almost as long as the fingers themselves. He thought such long nails showed that he had always been so rich and so important that he had never had to work with his hands. These silver thimble-like shields he had worn on the ends of his fingers to keep his precious long nails from breaking. Scholar Shih in the Court of Learning also wore his fingernails long.

From her treasure cabinet the Old Old One had taken out dainty fans with fair maidens and pretty country scenes painted upon their coverings of thin silk. She had shown the children old coins, bits of clear yellow amber, and other curios which she usually kept shut away in this shining red cabinet.

Ah Shung was holding between his thumb and forefinger a small dark-colored ball with fine carving upon it. The Old Old One took a round piece of glass from a drawer in the red cabinet and handed it to the boy.

"Look at it through this glass-eye-which-sees-everything-larger," she said. "That, Ah Shung, is a peach seed, and the carving upon it shows Miss Lin, the Sea Goddess, saving some sailors during a storm."

With the aid of the strong magnifying glass the children could see clearly the tiny figure of the maiden and the boat with sailors inside it, riding over high curving waves. The carving was perfect. Not the smallest thing was missing. And it was all done on a peach stone hardly more than an inch long!

Their grandmother explained to Ah Shung and Yu Lang how the fruit stone carvers worked. She told them of the care with which this peach seed had been dried so that it should not crack or sprout. She pointed out a tiny hole in the carving through which the kernel might have been picked out. And she said she thought the cutting must have been done under a magnifying glass such as that which Ah Shung held in his hand.

"I wish it were larger, Lao Lao," Yu Lang said, gazing at the peach stone. "I should like to see better the face of the Sea Goddess."

Her grandmother opened another drawer in the red treasure cabinet and took out a tiny round bottle with flattened sides. She explained that she sometimes used it to carry a powder called "snuff" which she liked to breathe in through her nose. For that reason she called it her "nose-sniff-bottle." It was so small that it did not wholly cover the palm of Yu Lang's little hand.

The girl gave a cry of delight when she saw the picture which was painted upon the flat sides of the snuff bottle. It seemed to her even more wonderful than the carving on the peach stone. For the bottle was painted on the inside.

With his brush thrust through its narrow neck, some skillful artist had made a picture of a beautiful maiden which showed clear through the glass. As on the carved peach stone, the maiden stood near the sea and there were sailors in a boat riding over the waves.

"That maiden, too, is the Sea Goddess, Jade Flower," said the Old Old One. "Look at her through the glass-eye-which-sees-everything-larger and you will find that she was a fair maid as well as a good daughter."

"Will you tell us about her, Lao Lao?" asked Ah Shung, as he stood the wee bottle up in the center of the table where they could all see it.

"Yes, this is a good tale for you to remember," the Old Old One said. "It happened like this. Hundreds of years ago, on the shores of the Eastern Sea, there lived a fisher family named Lin. Their daughter, whom they loved like precious jade, was the most dutiful maiden on all the seacoast. Each morning she rose early to cook breakfast for her parents. Each day she helped her father and her two brothers make ready for their journey out on the ocean, and she always went with them to their boats to wish them 'good wind and good water.'

"While the men were away fishing, the fair daughter of the Lin family stayed inside her walls, helping her mother with the household tasks, with spinning and weaving, and with preparing the meals. And not one single day did she forget to send up prayers to heaven upon sweet smoke from incense, asking the Jade Emperor to bless her dear parents.

"One day as Miss Lin sat with her mother at the midday meal she began to feel sleepy. Try as she would to keep awake, she fell into deep slumber, and as she slept she dreamed a strange dream. She thought that the five dragon brothers who live under the ocean were angry. They are marvelous beasts, these kings of the sea. More than a mile long they are. When they lash their tails mountains fall down, and the waves rise so high that they almost touch the sky. When the sea dragons fly up into the heavens hurricanes sweep across the land.

"In her dream on this day Miss Lin saw a mighty storm rage over the ocean. She saw her father and her two brothers in their little boats, tossing and tossing upon the angry waves. She rushed to the seashore. She waded out through the water. She reached forth and caught hold of the rope which was fastened to the bow of her father's boat. Quickly she put this between her teeth and then stretched forth her hands again to seize the ropes that were tied to the boats of her brothers.

"In her sleep the Lin maiden began to groan and to cry as she dreamed she was dragging the three boats toward the shore. Her mother, alarmed by her daughter's distress, shook her in order to wake her and to find out what the matter might be. In her dream Miss Lin heard her mother's voice calling her and she opened her mouth to answer. In a flash the rope slipped from between her teeth and her father's boat sank under the waves.

" 'O my mother, I have had a terrible nightmare,' the

girl said when she awoke. And she told how she had not yet reached the shore when the rope of her father's boat had slipped from her mouth.

"That night, on their return from the sea, the two brothers brought sad tidings to the house of the Lins. Their father's boat had been lost they said, and they feared he had gone to the Sea Dragon's palace. Poor Miss Lin blamed herself for the misfortune, for not having saved her father as she had saved her two brothers. She ran out of the house and down to the seashore, where she plunged into the waters in search of the lost one.

"None of her family ever met her again on the earth. But her brothers and other sailors often saw her out on the sea. They said she appeared whenever a storm was near, and that each time her figure was seen, seamen reached the shore safely.

"In later times, my children, a rich mandarin was once traveling upon the broad ocean when a great storm arose. The night was dark. The waves rose mountain high. He feared he was lost. Then out of the darkness there shone a bright point of light. It moved ahead of his boat, guiding it safely to a small island. When the mandarin asked the island folk what that light could have been, they were quick to reply that it was the lantern of Miss Lin, who protected all on the sea.

"Boatmen always paint eyes upon each side of their bows," the Old Old One told the children. "That is wise, because if the boats have no eyes, how can they see, and if they cannot see, how should they know where to go? But on a night of black darkness those eyes do little good. Many a sailor has called on Miss Lin to hold her lantern before him to show him the way. And all wise boatmen carry with them on their ships a small statue of this Sea Goddess. She usually stands between two fierce-looking generals whose names mean Eyes-Like-a-Cat and Ears-Sharp-As-the-Wind. And very good helpers such generals can be on a dark stormy night."

XXIX

SIMPLE SENG AND THE PARROT

Aʜ sʜᴜɴɢ! Ah Shung! Where are you, Bear Boy?" the Old Old One called to her grandson, as if he were out in the courtyard rather than in her own room. The boy was sitting on a low stool, gazing out of the open door at the white clouds that floated across the clear autumn sky. There was an absent look in his eyes, as if his thoughts were upon something far, far away.

"Excuse me, please, Lao Lao," he said with a start. "I was just thinking of our picnic for the Festival of Climbing High Places." Ah Shung was looking ahead to the Ninth Day of the Ninth Moon when the Lings, like their neighbors, always spent the day in the hills in the neighborhood of their city.

"And I suppose your spirit was already out on the mountainside above our family grave mounds," the old woman said, smiling down at the boy. The Lings believed that their souls often left their bodies. Each night when they slept and when dreams filled their minds, they thought they actually made voyages to far places and even to the Heavenly Kingdom itself. Grandmother Ling would not permit the nurses to move any of the children after they had fallen asleep, for she feared that their spirits might not be able to find their bodies again if they were not just where they had left them.

"It is not well for our souls to stay too long away," the Old Old One said thoughtfully, "but, at the same time, good often comes of the journeys they make. That was so with Simple Seng. Have I told you about him?"

"No, Lao Lao, we do not know that story," Yu Lang replied.

"Well, it is a strange tale, and I will tell it to you now, so that Ah Shung shall not long too much for the hills. In ancient times there lived a young man who was both well schooled and well mannered. It was only because he believed everything that was told him and because he took jesting words so seriously that his friends often nicknamed him 'Simple Seng.' He was timid and shy, especially when womenfolk were about, and when his girl cousins spoke to him he would blush fiery red.

"Now, in the same city where Sheng lived, there was a rich mandarin who had a daughter, Yen Chun, who was known far and wide for her beauty and cleverness. But she was known also as being very particular. She was quite old enough to be married, but her parents could not seem to find a husband that pleased her.

"Simple Seng was the subject of many a joke among the young men at the city teahouses. They found pleasure in the serious manner with which he received every word of advice, no matter how absurd it might be. One day, as they were discussing the beauty of the mandarin's daughter, they said to Seng, 'It is time you were married, good brother. Why do you not ask for the hand of lovely Yen Chun?' And they laughed among themselves at the thought of how that clever maid would receive a proposal from such a simple fellow as Seng.

"As usual, the young man took their words as if they had been spoken in earnest. He persuaded his father to send a go-between to ask for Yen Chun as his bride. But Seng was not rich and for this reason the mandarin quickly refused his request. Just as the go-between was leaving the guest hall he came upon the mandarin's daughter herself.

" 'Flower of Spring,' he said, bowing low, 'my errand inside your gate was to ask your hand in marriage for the excellent young man, Seng, of whom you may have heard.

He is a good youth. He knows well the sayings of the ancient scholars. He is handsome to look upon, his only blemish being a sixth finger on his left hand.'

"Now Yen Chun had heard of Seng. She knew he was shy and she did not think he would please her. So she dismissed the go-between with a jesting reply, 'Tell Seng,' she said, 'that I could never wed a man with six fingers.'

"The go-between repeated the maiden's words to Simple Seng, who at once called for a knife and chopped off his sixth finger. When the wound had healed nicely, he sent the man back again to the mandarin's house.

"Again Yen Chun made an excuse to the go-between. 'Tell Seng,' she said now, 'that I could never marry a man who took a joke so seriously.'

"This time the poor youth understood that she had been making fun of him, and he comforted himself by thinking that she would probably not have made him a good wife at all. But it happened then, as now, that on the Ninth Day of the Ninth Moon each family went forth to picnic on the hills and to tidy their grave mounds. In the crowds on the highway Seng and his brothers caught a glimpse of the lovely maiden, Yen Chun. So great was her beauty that the youth fell more deeply in love with her than ever.

"While the other young men were exclaiming about her raven-black hair and her skin fair as a flower, Seng said not a word. He gazed spellbound at her graceful figure that swayed like a young bamboo as she walked over the fields. He grew more and more thoughtful, and into his eyes there came a faraway look such as yours had just now, Ah Shung. When the day was ended, he had fallen into such a deep trance that his brothers had to take him home and put him to bed.

"For many days Simple Seng lay lost in slumber. He did not open his eyes. He seemed to hear nothing. When his mother tried to rouse him for his meals he would murmur, 'Pray go away. I am with the lovely Yen Chun.' For it seemed to him that, instead of returning home on the Day of Climbing High Places, he had followed Yen Chun. With her he had entered the mandarin's gate and had been received in her apartment.

"Indeed, so it seemed also to Yen Chun, my little ones. Each night dreams came to the maiden, and in them she met a handsome young man with a serious face who told her his name was Seng. But she said nothing to anyone, for it was not seemly for a young maiden like her to think so much about a young man.

"As the days went on and Seng did not rouse himself from his sleep his parents grew worried. 'Our son's life is in danger,' his mother said to his father. 'His soul drifts halfway between the earth and the heavens. We must send for a priest to call it back to his body.'

"From the name of the maiden, which the young man kept muttering his father knew where Seng's spirit might be, and he asked the mandarin for permission to send the priests into his courts to call it forth. 'How can your son's spirit be inside our wall?' the mandarin said. 'We do not have the pleasure of the young gentleman's acquaintance. We have not even seen him.' You see, my dear ones, he knew nothing of the meetings of Yen Chun and Simple Seng in the world of dreams.

"But the mandarin gave his permission, and the priest wrote out his prayers and placed them inside a round metal box which was set on the end of a stick like a wheel on its axle. He twirled the prayer wheel around and around. It made a clattering noise which the gods could not fail to notice, and as it spun the priest called the name of the youth again and again. Yen Chun who had heard of the priest's coming, had no doubt but that the young man for whom his prayer wheel was turning was the one she had been meeting in the land of dreams, and her heart was moved.

"At the priest's call, the spirit of Seng returned to his body. He awoke. He rose from his bed and went on about his duties and pleasures. But he took little interest in anything save his thoughts of Yen Chun. His only wish was to see the fair maiden again.

"The youth finally bribed the mandarin's gateman to tell him when Yen Chun would go abroad in the city, and one day when she was on her way to pray in the temple he stood by the highway to see her pass. Through the peephole in the side of her sedan chair the young maiden's eyes fell upon him, and she even dared to lift the corner of its curtain the better to see him. When she found that this handsome youth was the Seng of her dreams, her heart beat with joy.

"Again and again Seng tried to send his spirit to visit Yen Chun as before. But the dreams did not come. Then one day, as he lay on his couch thinking of her, his small brother brought into his room the body of a parrot which had only just died. At once the young man thought to himself, 'If my spirit could enter the body of this bird, how easily I could fly to the court of Yen Chun.'

"And, quick as the thought had flashed through his mind, he fell back on his bed and the parrot moved its wings. The bird rose from the floor and flew out of the window. Straight as the string of a kite borne on a strong wind, my children, that parrot flew to the window of the lovely Yen Chun. It lit on her wrist and caressed her hand with its beak. The girl was delighted with the tame bird, and she was about to fasten a little chain round its leg when it began to speak.

"'There is no need to chain me, Spring Flower,' said the parrot. 'I am Seng, whose only wish is to stay here with you. It was I who sent the go-between to ask you to marry me. It was I who stood by the roadside to see your chair pass.'

"'Your devotion has touched my heart, O Elder Brother,' the maid said politely. 'But since you are now a bird, how can we be wed?'

"It would be enough for me to spend my days by your side,' the parrot replied. 'I do not ask for more.'

"Yen Chun fed the parrot from her own hand. He perched on her shoulder and he slept at her feet. The maiden became so fond of the bird that she was unhappy away from him. Indeed, she loved him so dearly that she wished that he was not a parrot at all. She greatly desired that he should become once more the handsome young man she had seen from her chair on the way to the temple.

"The girl sent one of the servants to the house of his father to ask whether Seng was living or dead. The man brought back word that Seng was sleeping as though in a deep trance. His life, the servant reported still hung between heaven and earth. Then Yen Chun lifted the parrot up on her finger and she rubbed its smooth feathers.

" 'Go back to your own body, O Splendid Spirit,' she said. 'Become a young man again and I vow I will wed you.' The parrot cocked its head first on one side, then on the other, as if it were thinking. Then it swooped down upon one of Yen Chun's tiny red shoes that lay on a chair. Holding the bit of embroidered satin in his beak, it flew out of the window. The maiden called to the bird to bring her shoe back to her, but it did not listen.

"In the house of Seng, his mother and father, his brothers and sisters were all gathered about the young man's body as it lay on the bed. They were weeping because Seng did not move and because he would not speak to them. Suddenly, to their surprise, a parrot flew in through the window, lit on the bed, and fell over dead. And a tiny red shoe which the bird had held in its beak

The maiden called to the bird to bring her shoe back to her, but it did not listen

dropped to the floor. At the same moment the body of the young man stirred. To his family's great joy, he sat up and spoke.

"Just then there came a knocking at the gate. It was the maid of Yen Chun, come to ask if her mistress's red shoe was there. 'Go back to your mistress,' Seng said to the servant. 'Tell her that the red shoe stands for a promise. When that promise is kept she shall have her shoe back.'

"The lovely Yen Chun told her parents of the strange dreams and of the enchanted parrot, and she vowed she would wed no husband but Seng. Her father, the mandarin, did not want to give his daughter to a young man who had so few coins in his money box. 'But that is not the worst, my daughter,' he said. 'This young man is not only poor. He is simple besides.'

" 'Simple he may be, but he is the one I will wed,' the maiden declared. 'If you refuse I will throw myself in the lake and you will see me no more.'

"There was nothing for her father to do then but consent. The lucky day was chosen by the fortune teller and the wedding took place. So happy was Seng, with Yen Chun for his bride, that he learned how to laugh. He could jest with the merriest, and from his wedding day on no one thought of calling him Simple Seng. So clever and wise did he become that they spoke of him instead as Seng the Sage."

XXX

THE OLD OLD ONE'S BIRTHDAY

LAO LAO'S BIRTHDAY is as exciting as the New Year,"
Ah Shung said to his sister, Yu Lang. They were watching
visitors laden with parcels step in through the Moon Gate
and walk across the Courtyard of Politeness to the guest
hall.

"It is even better," Yu Lang replied. "For today there

will be not only feasting and firecrackers and guests bringing presents, but plays on the stage which they have set up here in the courtyard."

Many days had been spent in making ready for this great occasion, when the head of the Ling household should reach the age of seventy years. As much care had been taken to clean each crack and corner of every low house inside the gray walls as at the time of the New Year. The very stones of the courtyards shone with the scouring they had received, and chrysanthemums bloomed in the Garden of Sweet Smells as though the flowers, too, wished to please the Old Old One on her birthday.

Like everyone else, Ah Shung and Yu Lang had on new suits of soft silk. The Old Old One herself was splendid in a long gown of silver-gray satin lined with soft squirrel fur. She was wearing her best carved jade earrings and bracelets, and in her coil of gray hair was a pin of pure gold, set with precious pearls. To look at her calm face one would never guess how much the old woman was enjoying this day when all the members of her family, from near and from far, had come to do her honor. Even her daughters, who now lived inside the walls of their husband's families, once more passed through the bright red gate of the Lings.

The two children, Ah Shung and Yu Lang, had gone early to give Lao Lao birthday greetings. While she was still having her breakfast in her room, Yu Lang bowed before her and handed her a gift which she had made with her own hands. It was a square of red silk upon which, with her older sister to guide her, the little girl had embroidered a peach-of-long-life. Lao Lao declared she would prize it more highly than the finest roll of shining satin which she might receive during the day.

Ah Shung also bowed before his grandmother. With both hands outstretched he handed her a scroll. Upon its narrow white paper the boy himself had made with his brush and his ink paste perfect black word pictures which stood for "Long Life and Happiness." The children were proud indeed when Grandmother Ling ordered her maids to take their gifts to the guest hall where visitors might see them.

Theirs were only two of the hundred or more presents that were spread out upon the red-covered table in the great reception room in the Courtyard of Politeness. There the Old Old One sat to receive the members of her family, who kowtowed before her as they wished her well. There she welcomed the stream of guests who poured in and out of the red gate. Tables spread with good things to eat and to drink were there for their pleasure, and all the day through the sound of pleasant chatter filled the huge room and rose to the high rafters under its curving roof.

In the afternoon actors from the city, dressed in gay-colored costumes, strutted back and forth across the little stage which had been built out of doors for the birthday plays. How the children enjoyed the music of the players, who beat their drums and clashed their cymbals and played on their flutes! They listened spellbound to the chanting voices of the men who took the parts of princesses and queens, as well as of mandarins, soldiers, and beggars in the short one-act plays.

The day passed all too quickly. At the birthday table in the family hall Ah Shung and Yu Lang, like the other members of the family and guests, emptied one bowl after another. Chicken and duck, pork dumplings and rice, spicy salt vegetables, and thin long-life noodles were set down before them. There were fruits of many kinds and sweet cakes on whose tops, done in red sugar, were the word pictures that stood for "long life," "riches," and "joy." Everyone ate until he could no longer swallow. Then the chopsticks were laid neatly across each empty bowl and the maid servants passed around hot steaming towels so that all the crumbs might be wiped from faces and hands.

"Now that the guests have departed," Lao Lao said in the evening after the feast and the fireworks, "I must give thanks once again to the God of Long Life." The family followed her to the guest hall where a small table, covered with red silk, had been set like an altar before a painting that hung on the wall. The picture showed an old man riding upon a stag, with a bat flying above his head. The stag and the bat, the Old Old One had often explained to the children, stood for good luck and happiness. The peach which the old man held in one hand and the gourd and the scroll which hung from his staff were the symbols for long life.

A kneeling-cushion had been placed before the red altar table, upon which red candles burned. Ah Shung and Yu Lang were much interested in little images of two old men, about six inches high, which had been placed on either side of the small bronze incense urn in the center of the table.

The Old Old One lighted fresh incense sticks and knelt down on the cushion to give thanks for the seventy years she had been permitted to dwell upon earth. Her eldest son followed. He prayed to the god to give her many years more with which to brighten the lives of all in this household. His wife and the other members of the family, according to age, took their turn on the kneeling-cushion, the children kowtowing as well as the grownups and praying for long life for their beloved grandmother.

When all honor had been paid to the God of Long Life, the Old Old One opened the last of her gifts. There were rolls of silk, thick enough to make several new gowns. There was a tiny white metal hand-warmer in which bits of charcoal could be burned and which Grandmother Ling could cuddle in her cold hands or thrust inside her robe when the time of the "Big Cold" should bring bitter winds in through the cracks. Pieces of jewelry, candies and cakes in bright red lacquer boxes, books, fans, and porcelain bowls, and other gifts of many kinds covered the red satin top of the long birthday table. Most of the fruits that had been sent to the Old Old One on this day were peaches, both fresh and preserved, which reminded the children of the long-life fruit from the tree in the mountains of Kun Lun.

As the family sat about the guest hall, talking of the events of the day, Ah Shung found a chance to ask his grandmother about the two little old men upon the red altar before which they had kowtowed.

"Those, Little Bear," the old woman replied, "are the Old Man of the North whose nickname is 'Age-As-Great-As-the-Mountains,' and his brother, the Old Man of the South, whom men sometimes call 'Happiness-Deep-As-the-Sea.' We put them on the altar of the God of Long Life and we say prayers to them, too, in the hope that they may lengthen our years as they did those of young Tong.

"Who was Tong, Lao Lao?" Yu Lang asked eagerly.

"He was a lad who lived long, long ago, Little Precious," Lao Lao answered. "One day as he walked along the city street he came upon a crowd gathered about the table of a famous fortune teller whose name was Kwan Lo. Some fortune tellers have trained little birds to pick out one card from among many in order to answer a question which has been put to them. Others use slender sticks, with the answers written upon them, which they shake up in a bamboo cup and from which they choose one. But this man was no ordinary fortune teller, my children. He had no such things to help him. He read the future himself in the faces of those who came to him for guidance.

"Tong watched Kwan Lo examine the noses and the eyes, the mouths and the ears, of his curious customers. He saw him peer at their cheekbones, their teeth, and their eyebrows. And he heard the wise words that came from the man's lips. He was so impressed that he could not forbear to ask questions himself.

" 'Drop into my ear the pearls of your wisdom, Honored Sir,' Tong said when his turn had come and when he had laid down his coins on the table. The fortune teller examined the lad's face with great earnestness. Then he shook his head and a sad look came into his eyes.

" 'Ai-yah, young gentleman,' he said with a note of sorrow in his voice. 'It is too bad that a fine fellow like you should die so soon.'

" 'What do you say, sir?' Tong cried. 'Am I going to die?'

" 'When the sun sets on the night of your nineteenth birthday, my son, the gods will have plucked the flower of your life,' Kwan Lo said to the youth.

" 'And I am eighteen even now,' poor Tong wailed, as he hurried away to his home to tell his parents of his misfortune. His father and mother were greatly distressed, and they went with the lad to consult Kwan Lo again.

" 'There is no help for it,' the fortune teller declared. 'In the great Book of Life it is written that you shall die when you reach the age of nineteen. I see the page clearly. The only advice I can give you would be to go in search of the Old Man of the North who guards that Book. I can tell you where you may find him and what you should do. But the outcome will depend on how you yourself please the Old Man of the North.

" 'Heap two plates with fresh deer-meat, well cooked and

well seasoned, and take with you two bottles of wine,' Kwan Lo told the youth. 'Climb to the top of yonder mountain, and there you will find two very old men playing chess. Do not disturb them, but set the plates and the bottles within reach of their hands. Then wait till they speak to you before you ask for their help.'

"Tong did as the fortune teller directed. With his basket on his arm, he climbed the high mountain. And when he reached the top he came upon the two very old men whom Kwan Lo had described. They were bent over their chess-board, Ah Shung, just as you and I when we play on rainy days. Their eyes were fixed upon their black and white armies. They did not look up, for each one was intent on surrounding his enemy and winning the game.

"Those two chess players, my dear ones, were the Old Man of the South, who keeps a record of births and who brings so much happiness, and the Old Man of the North in whose great Book of Life the time of everyone's death is written down. Tong remembered the words of Kwan Lo, the fortune teller, and even though he was impatient, he stood very still until the game was finished. He did not forget, however, to set the plate of deer-meat and the bottles of wine where the old men could reach them.

"But even a chess game comes to an end sometime. When this one was finished the old men seemed hungry. They reached out and took the deer-meat from the plates and they drained the wine from the bottles. It was only when they leaned back with the sighs of content that come from a full stomach that they noticed poor Tong.

" 'Who is this?' demanded the Old Man of the North as he caught sight of the lad.

"It is an unworthy youth, Heavenly Sage,' said Tong, 'who has come to beg your help. Kwan Lo, the fortune teller, declares that my years are numbered to only nineteen. I am even now eighteen. If you cannot aid me, I shall die before the New Year.'

" 'Let me see! Let me see!' the Old Man of the North said, setting his spectacles on his nose and opening his great Book of Life. He turned over the leaves until he came to Tong's name. 'Yes,' he said, pointing with his old wrinkled finger, 'so it is written. Look, here it says 'Tong' and there it says 'nineteen.' Too bad, too bad! But I will have pity upon you, good youth, since you brought us such a fine feast. Beside your name I will change one of the figures, so that you shall have many more birthdays on which you may offer me thanks.'

"The Old Man of the North took up his writing brush, and with careful strokes he changed the figure one into a nine, so that the length of Tong's years read ninety-nine instead of nineteen. The young man's heart was filled with happiness. He fell to his knees and kowtowed again and again to the Old Man of the North. As he was taking his leave, the Old Man spoke to him thus: 'Say to that fortune-teller, Kwan Lo, that he did wrong to tell you how long you should live. Bid him take care not to give away our secrets again. The time set by heaven should not be known upon earth. Either it gives too much joy or it gives too much sadness. And you, young gentleman, keep what we have done for you to yourself. We do not want every man, woman, and child rushing up our mountainside to beg us to change the figures beside their names in the Book of Life.' "

When the Old Old One had ended her story, little Yu Lang rose from her seat and toddled on her bound feet to the side of her grandmother's chair. She put her small hand timidly upon the silver gray silk of the Old Old One's gown and she looked up into her face.

"I shall pray to the Old Man of the North that he will let you live also for ninety-nine years, Lao Lao," she said. Tears filled her soft black eyes as she remembered the smooth wooden coffin which her grandmother kept so carefully, ready, in one of the rooms of her apartment. The little girl and her brother and the other children inside the bright red gate of the Lings truly hoped that their Lao Lao would live for a long time. They could not imagine what their days would be like if they had no Old Old One to love them and teach them and tell them splendid stories about wonderful things that happened long, long ago.

Other TUT BOOKS available:

UNBEATEN TRACKS IN JAPAN: An Account of Travels in the Interior Including Visits to the Aborigines of Yezo and the Shrine of Nikko *by Isabella L. Bird*

ZILCH! The Marine Corps' Most Guarded Secret *by Roy Delgado*

Please order from your bookstore or write directly to:

CHARLES E. TUTTLE CO., INC.
Suido 1-chome, 2–6, Bunkyo-ku, Tokyo 112

or:

CHARLES E. TUTTLE CO., INC.
Rutland, Vermont 05701 U.S.A.